What she

A way to ta............ off the snow. And off the
sexy and disarming man lying beside April in the
dark. "We could talk about the job I have to do
instead."

"We could," Weston said easily. "But since you're
sharing my roof tonight, and I climbed all this way
to save your lovely hide, I think the information is
going to cost you."

"Is that so?"

"Definitely." His voice took on a silky note as he
skimmed a touch up her arm to her shoulder.

Her heart rate doubled.

"What are you suggesting?" she asked, with a hint
more breathlessness than she would have liked.

"I think a kiss per question would be fair."

April felt a wave of heat, as if someone switched off
the snow and turned on a fireplace...and that heat
was the last thing she needed.

* * *

Rule Breaker by Joanne Rock is part of the
Dynasties: Mesa Falls series.

Dear Reader,

Beautiful heroine April Stephens is poised and lovely on the outside, but her carefully cultivated exterior hides dark secrets and an uncomfortable past. Her efforts to be a good daughter while still striving for an independent, successful future not only inspired me, they reminded me that so many people we meet in life are hiding hurts we never see. Characters like this help me remember to be a kinder human to the people around me.

I did send April a worthy hero, however! Weston Rivera thoroughly captured my heart in a scene from December's *The Rival*, when April saw him quiet a horse. His calm demeanor and obvious comfort with animals communicated so much about him to her—and me—right away.

I hope you enjoy their story, and please do join me for Gabe's book next month when *Heartbreaker* comes to Mesa Falls!

Happy reading,

Joanne Rock

JOANNE ROCK

———

RULE BREAKER

To Theo Nestor, whose creativity never stops growing! You've inspired me as a mother and a teacher and now as a writer and an artist.

DESIRE

ISBN-13: 978-1-335-20891-0

Rule Breaker

Copyright © 2020 by Joanne Rock

This edition published by arrangement with Harlequin Books S.A.

For questions and comments about the quality of this book, please contact us at CustomerService@Harlequin.com.

Harlequin Enterprises ULC
22 Adelaide St. West, 40th Floor
Toronto, Ontario M5H 4E3, Canada
www.Harlequin.com

Printed in U.S.A.

Joanne Rock credits her decision to write romance after a book she picked up during a flight delay engrossed her so thoroughly that she didn't mind at all when her flight was delayed two more times. Giving her readers the chance to escape into another world has motivated her to write over eighty books for a variety of Harlequin series.

Books by Joanne Rock

Harlequin Desire

The McNeill Magnates

The Magnate's Mail-Order Bride
The Magnate's Marriage Merger
His Accidental Heir
Little Secrets: His Pregnant Secretary
Claiming His Secret Heir
For the Sake of His Heir
The Forbidden Brother
Wild Wyoming Nights
One Night Scandal

Dynasties: Mesa Falls

The Rebel
The Rival
Rule Breaker

Visit her Author Profile page at Harlequin.com, or joannerock.com, for more titles.

You can also find Joanne Rock on Facebook, along with other Harlequin Desire authors, at Facebook.com/harlequindesireauthors!

Mesa Falls

The Key Players

Mesa Falls Ranch, Montana's premier luxury corporate retreat, got its start when a consortium bought the property.

The Owners

Weston Rivera, rancher

Miles Rivera, rancher

Gage Striker, investment banker

Desmond Pierce, casino resort owner

Alec Jacobsen, game developer

Jonah Norlander, technology company CEO

What do the owners have in common?

They all went to Dowdon School, where they were students of the late Alonzo Salazar.

The Salazars

Alonzo Salazar (dec.), retired teacher at Dowdon School, CEO of Salazar Media

Devon Salazar, copresident, Salazar Media, Alonzo's son

Marcus Salazar, copresident, Salazar Media, Alonzo's son, Devon's half brother

As these key players converge, dark secrets come to light in Big Sky Country...

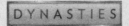

Where family loyalties and passions collide...

One

Maybe a wiser man would have blocked her number.

Weston Rivera gripped his cell phone tighter as he paced from his home office into the sunken family room. He knew he couldn't pretend he hadn't seen the text from a certain sexy private investigator he really needed to avoid.

The sun was already setting outside, but he could still discern the faint outline of the Bitterroot Mountains framed through the floor-to-ceiling windows. The hulking, irregular peaks were partially shrouded by an incoming storm.

Swearing to himself, he peered back down at the message on his screen.

Any tips for navigating the Northeast Couloir trail?
Just made camp but hope to summit in the morning.

Did he have tips?

As a proficient climber and mountain-rescue volunteer, he sure as hell had advice for April Stephens,
the smoking-hot financial forensics expert who was
an unwelcome guest at Mesa Falls Ranch. She should
have never climbed a class-four trail in the winter
by herself in the kind of weather brewing out there.

Too bad she hadn't asked him *before* she started
up the mountain.

He'd really thought he'd dodged April for good.
The last time she'd cornered him at the ranch office, he'd made it abundantly clear that he had no
comment about her investigation into the finances
of Alonzo Salazar, a frequent guest of the retreat
Weston owned with his brother and four other partners. Salazar had been a friend and mentor to all of
them since they were teenagers. And he'd been there
when a devastating accident had ended in a classmate's death. Weston wasn't about to speculate on
what the man did with his money. Loyalty wasn't
something Weston took lightly.

Yet he hadn't blocked the investigator's number
after that meeting, which had paved the way for today's text message.

Was she baiting him? Looking for a way to re-
start their conversation and dig up dirt for her investigation? Or was she genuinely contemplating that

climb? He'd heard from one of the trail guides that she'd visited a local outfitter for gear when she'd first arrived, so he wasn't surprised she wanted to get out into the mountains. But a day trip was tough enough in the winter, even on the easier peaks.

Cursing again, he dropped down to the leather sofa close to the fireplace. A log popped and shifted, sending a shower of sparks against the screen. How should he respond? Obviously, he didn't want her trekking back down the mountain by herself in the dark. But with the weather worsening by the minute, spending the night up there could be hazardous too. He knew he had an overdeveloped sense of caution where others were concerned, even if he was a risk taker himself. That cautious streak probably stemmed from the tragedy that had bound his fate to Alonzo Salazar's more than a decade ago.

Where are you?

He banged out the words with more force than necessary, already knowing where this conversation was going to lead.

She replied with a link. Map coordinates like any good hiker would use, showing her exact position.

His chest eased a bit at first. If she knew about tricks like that, she surely had some solid climbing experience. Clearly, she understood the importance of knowing her location at all times. But as he zoomed in closer on the map to see where she had made camp, the tightness in his chest returned.

And then tripled.

Because April wasn't camping in one of the safer spots like Gem Lake or Baker's Lake. Instead, she wasn't all that far from the Northeast Couloir. A notorious avenue for avalanche activity.

It didn't matter how experienced a climber she was or whether she knew the risks. She was a guest of his ranch. Someone he felt responsible for. Now that she'd specifically asked for his advice on this ill-advised venture, he had no choice. He had to help.

Stay there. Keep phone on. Don't light a fire. I'm on my way.

She might not be happy to see him. But Weston didn't particularly care. Shoving his phone in his pocket, he took the stairs two at a time up to his bedroom to dress for a climb that he hoped like hell wouldn't turn into a rescue effort. Just the thought of it turned his blood icy, and he hadn't even set foot out of the house yet.

He already had one catastrophic event on his conscience. He couldn't survive a second.

"'I'm on my way'?" April Stephens read aloud from the text she'd received almost an hour ago.

Tucked in the sleeping bag laid over an insulated pad she'd rented from the local outfitter, April still couldn't fight off the chill from her climb as she shut off her screen to save the phone battery. The shiver up her spine didn't have anything to do with the knowledge that Weston Rivera, the rich and powerful rancher who'd been dodging her attempts to speak with him, was on his way to see her. The memory of his hazel eyes smoked through her, even though the last time she'd confronted him he had threatened to call security to have her escorted out of his office.

Why was he hiking up here now? In the dark?

Wind howled off nearby Trapper Peak and tore at her one-ply tent, making her wonder if her shelter had been the right choice for this trip. It was lighter, which had allowed her to bring the additional gear necessary for a winter climb. But she hadn't counted on this level of heavy gusts. She'd thought she'd read up on the Bitterroot Mountains thoroughly, and she'd checked the weather before she started hiking, but somewhere during her trek this afternoon, the conditions had shifted dramatically.

That was part of the reason she'd reached out to Weston Rivera, who was well known around Mesa Falls Ranch for his mountaineering skills. Of course, there was more to her agenda than getting tips on the mountain. She'd hoped maybe their shared interest in climbing would spark a dialogue. Give her another chance at wrangling some answers from him regarding a case that was thwarting her at every turn.

She most definitely hadn't expected him to drop everything to come to her. But the fact that he would do that—even though he'd made it obvious he wanted to avoid her—caused her to wonder if she'd overestimated her skills in making this climb on her own.

Guilt nipped at her nearly as hard as the bitter wind. Did he think she was in danger? She should have made it clear that she had a reasonable amount of climbing experience. She'd even tackled this mountain once before, just not this particular trail. She never did anything without studying all the angles first. It was a quality that made her excel at her job as a financial forensics investigator.

As soon as she'd received his cryptic text, she'd messaged him back a bunch of question marks in reply. Then she'd sent him an assurance she was fine, but she hadn't heard anything else from him, prompting her to believe he really might be climbing a mountain in the middle of the night.

Unzipping the tent a couple of inches, she peered out into the inky blackness. She still wore her parka for sleeping, but she'd taken off her boots and gloves for the night. She felt more than saw the swirl of snow kicking up outside, the tiny flakes peppering her cheeks in a frigid blast. A gust of wind whistled past her ears, lifting the inner tent roof and whipping the outer fabric so hard she feared it might rip. The snow was coming down faster now. The powdery base had scaled the tent walls at least an inch since she'd pitched the shelter.

A little bubble of panic rose inside her at the feeling of being closed in. She'd been drawn to mountain climbing as a teen to escape the suffocating home life with her mother, who was then in the early stages of a hoarding disorder. April had climbed to find fresh air and freedom, a place without walls of crap threatening to fall on her everywhere she looked. Now, as an adult, she lived in a beautifully spare home of her own, but she felt the urge to climb whenever stress built from dealing with her mom. April still tried to help, making scheduled trips over to the house where she'd grown up to make sure her mom was still going to counseling and hadn't fired the professional organizer who came through once a month. Her mother's house would always be cluttered—to put it mildly—but at least things were at a habitable level.

Even knowing that she'd done all she could to make her mother's disease manageable didn't stem the memories of how bad things had been—and how quickly her mom could relapse. Which was why April hiked until her mind was clear again.

So now, as she took in the way the snow covered the lower zipper on the tent, almost as if it was going to block her exit, her heart pounded fast. Her face heated despite the cold, a sweaty fear crawling up her scalp and making her see pinpricks of light in front of her eyes.

Light?

Frowning, she focused on the glow bobbing in the blizzard. As it grew closer, the bright spot seemed to rise in the sky.

Coming toward her.

"April." A man's hoarse voice carried on the wind just as a dark shadow took shape in front of her.

Weston—wearing a headlamp—was stalking up the trail.

"Here," she called back, her softer voice mostly lost in the wind. She found her flashlight just inside the tent and flipped the switch so he could see her.

As he entered the circle of illumination from her torch, she could tell how much conditions had worsened. He was covered with snow, from his jacket and pants to his helmet and balaclava. Even his goggles were coated. Knowing that he'd trekked through this weather to get to her filled her with new alarm.

He crouched down near the entrance to the tent, his broad shoulders blocking the wind. Close enough to touch. He raked his goggles up and switched off the headlamp. His hazel eyes locked on hers, his demeanor as serious as the last time they'd met when he'd threatened to call security on her if she didn't leave his office. Only now, he looked concerned.

Worried, even.

"We need to move you," he told her, his gaze never wavering. "Carefully and quickly."

Confused, she shook her head. "I don't understand."

"You're in a well-documented avalanche corridor." He spoke the words clearly and almost kindly, as if he weren't talking about the imminent possibility of a deadly accident. "And conditions are only going to deteriorate with this storm."

She recognized now what he was doing. He was speaking to her like a rescue worker. Like someone used to dealing with people in terrifying danger. That manner of his, as much as the words themselves, sent a cold ball of fear into the pit of her belly.

"Why—" Her breath stuck in her chest, and she couldn't breathe for a moment as panic spiraled into every corner of her body. "Why didn't you tell me in your text? I've just been sitting here…"

She peered around the tent, calculating how long it would take to put on her gear. Another sharp gust tore at the outer tent. She was pretty sure she heard the fabric tear.

"Look at me, April." He spoke patiently, his tone still kind even though she'd made a horrible mistake in coming up here. Risking her neck and his. "You were safer staying put than you would have been out there when you don't know the nuances of this trail. But I know this area like the back of my hand, and I'm going to take you to a safer location."

Nodding, she appreciated his calming presence while her mind raced. She had logged countless hours climbing in summer conditions, but not as many in the winter. One of her mentors back in Denver had told her that she should take an avalanche course, but she hadn't gotten to that stage yet. Hadn't known she'd need it for this peak so early in the winter. She felt foolish for endangering herself and—worse—Weston too.

He couldn't possibly know how much she hated

being in this position, feeling like she'd screwed up. Like she'd overlooked something important.

"Okay. Thank you." Swallowing back her fear, she focused on his hazel eyes, needing to believe he was as confident as he sounded. "I'll get my gear on."

He moved her out of harm's way quickly enough.

The knot of worry in Weston's chest eased a fraction with each step they took away from the gully where she'd pitched her tent for the night. Avalanches were a real danger in that ravine. He hadn't been a part of any rescue missions there, but there'd been another one ten years back that some of his team had experienced. Plus, he'd seen two avalanches with his own eyes on these peaks. Both had scared the hell out of him.

And conditions tonight were prime. He was so damned grateful he'd found her, and that she'd been safe. Whole.

The demons from his past had teeth, and they would still be gnawing on him when he closed his eyes tonight.

"Where are we going?" she called to him through the wind, her voice doubly muffled by her scarf.

They trudged side by side down the mountain, their pace slow in case of loose rocks under the snow. He'd offered her a second headlamp that he'd brought with him, but she had her own and wore it now. She'd been more prepared than he had anticipated, from her gear to her ease with packing quickly and efficiently.

She'd been scared, though. He'd read the fear easily in her body language from her blinking eyes and darting gaze to her jerky movements, signs that would have been clear even if he hadn't been trained to deal with frightened survivors. He'd done his best to calm her once they were out of the most dangerous area, but he could tell she was spooked. And he'd damn well been reassured this wasn't a setup on her part. She hadn't baited him out onto the mountain just for a chance to interrogate him about his dealings with Alonzo Salazar, the subject of her financial investigation.

She would have had to be a good actress to fake the fear he'd witnessed earlier. The flash of panic in her blue eyes. The tremor in her voice. Although with her goggles on now, he had fewer cues to how she was doing.

"There are safe campsites this way." They hadn't gone far from her original spot, since he wouldn't risk a fall in the dark in these harsh weather conditions, but they were out of the ravine and following a ridge he knew well.

"Shouldn't we get off the mountain?" she pressed, leaning closer to him as she spoke.

If he'd been alone—yes. He would have returned to the all-terrain vehicle he'd left at a trailhead. But he wouldn't risk it with April in tow. Sure, she seemed like she must be a strong climber on a regular day. But it was late; she had to be tired and most definitely stressed. Bottom line, he didn't trust her sure-footedness or her judgment and couldn't risk going any farther than necessary.

"Safer to make camp someplace I know will be protected until the storm passes." He pointed to a spot tucked out of the wind ahead of them. Between a secure rock ledge and sheltering trees, there was far less snow here. "I brought a big tent with the highest weather rating."

Stepping under the shelter of the ledge, he shed his backpack and unzipped it to dig out the gear. Only when he pulled off his gloves did he realize she'd stopped moving. A few steps behind him, she looked lost in the spotlight of his headlamp, snow almost reaching her knees.

She might have said something, but the words were lost in the wind.

Gesturing for her to come closer, he called, "I can't hear you."

He set his flashlight on the rock ledge so it shone down onto his backpack while April hopped down to join him. She wrenched off her goggles, taking her headlamp with them. He could see her blue eyes clearly now.

"You're staying?" she asked, the question huffing into the cold air between them. "With me?"

Maybe it was because she didn't seem frightened anymore. Or maybe it was because he knew they were out of danger here. But something in the way she asked reminded him how very appealing he found this woman. And how grateful he was that she was safe.

April Stephens had been a red-hot distraction from the first time he'd seen her. Then he'd discovered how good she was at her job as she started to uncover the long-kept secrets of his mentor. And tonight, he'd seen a grit in her that he never would have expected from a woman who looked like she'd be more at home on a glossy magazine cover than a Montana ranch—let alone on a mountaintop.

From the high cheekbones and delicate bone structure to her pillow-soft lips, she had an exquisite beauty that turned male heads. But better than that, she had a fiery determination that he admired, even if he'd been on the wrong side of it when they met.

"I didn't hike all this way in the dark only to leave you alone now, April." He couldn't have held back the flare of anticipation now if he tried. Not that he was going to seduce a woman he felt responsible for tonight. But he couldn't deny the sensual draw every time he was around her. "I'm not going anywhere."

"That's—kind of you." She didn't sound convinced of that, but at least her voice sounded stronger. Feistier. "But I have a tent of my own."

She was already wriggling out of the straps of her backpack, plunking it down in the snow while he found his ice ax, which doubled as a mallet to pound in the stakes.

"You've got a tear in yours," he reminded her. He'd heard the fabric shredding in the high gusts along the ravine before he'd helped her disassemble it. "Besides, this is meant for two people."

His shelter was state-of-the-art. Everest winds wouldn't take the thing down. Setup took less than two minutes since he was familiar with the equipment and accustomed to putting together a shelter in a hurry. He tossed his sleeping bag and insulated pad inside and then held the canvas flap door open for her.

She still clutched her own backpack uncertainly, wind whipping the ends of her hair that she hadn't taken time to tuck into her hat. Lips pursed, she studied him and seemed to weigh her options.

That's when the adrenaline letdown from the rescue mission kicked in, rushing through him in the form of sweet, sharp desire.

April must have been blinded by the snow-globe effect of white swirling between them, because she didn't seem to notice. She took a deep breath and crawled inside the tent, giving him a view of lush feminine curves that didn't do anything to put out the flames.

Swallowing back the sudden hunger for her, he ground his teeth while he watched her carefully remove her boots and leave them in the vestibule area. He tilted his face up to the snow, needing the cooling touch on his heated skin before he got anywhere near her.

No doubt about it, he was in for a long night ahead.

Two

The last time she checked, Weston Rivera didn't even *like* her, April reminded herself as she tucked deeper into her sleeping bag in the roomy, two-person tent he'd put up as fast as a magic trick. So it was foolish of her to think she felt any kind of spark between them.

Especially in the frigid cold, on a windy mountaintop, after he'd risked his own neck to save hers. If anything, he should be irritated with her. Surely she was imagining the hot, simmering sensation as he stripped off his snow-covered outer layer. She watched him by the light of the lantern he'd set on the ground. Even in the harsh, bluish glare, Weston was ruggedly handsome.

His dark blond hair was long, past the collar of the gray flannel shirt under his parka. A light brown scruff of whiskers covered his jaw, calling to her fingertips to test the texture. With powerful shoulders and hazel eyes a woman could lose herself in, Weston possessed far too much masculine appeal.

Maybe she was the one feeling all the heat. She'd probably imagined the answering hunger in his eyes, her emotions on edge after having to be rescued from her own poor decision making tonight. Which reminded her: she owed him an apology.

The words were on the tip of her tongue when his thigh brushed hers as he slid off his work pants with the bright yellow reflective stripes on the legs. He wore pants underneath them, of course, but there was something terribly intimate about him undressing an inch away from her. Even in a two-person tent, the space was narrow—just big enough for their sleeping bags, side by side. The contact made her thigh tingle.

"Won't you be cold?" she blurted, mostly to distract herself from the response she was having to him. She had kept most of her layers on, while her snow goggles, boots and outer waterproof mittens dried in the vestibule area. She even kept on a soft pair of inner gloves and the knit hat she'd worn under her ski hood.

She'd kept the inner fleece from her parka and the base layer of her ski pants too, since she'd shivered all the way over from the first campsite. She wasn't sure if it was a true physical chill or just a cold feeling she had in her belly from discovering she'd pitched a tent in an avalanche zone.

"No." Weston leaned back in the sleeping bag, so that he was almost lying down beside her. But first, he draped his discarded jacket on top of the sleeping bag, and then arranged his pants so they rested above his legs. "I use them like extra blankets. They're uncomfortable if I keep them on, since I carry a lot of gear in the pockets."

With the layers configured the way he wanted, he lifted the lantern and held it above her as he propped himself on one elbow. His breath huffed in the light as he spoke again. "Can I shut this down for the night?"

Her throat dried up at the sight of him so close. A rush of gratitude filled her that he'd done so much to help her and keep her safe tonight. But that appreciation was bound up with so many more complicated feelings. Conflict. Attraction. Regret that she'd put him in this position at all.

"Yes," she rasped on a husky breath. "I'm all set."

The memory of what he looked like in that moment—big strong arms, powerful chest and tender concern in his eyes—would be burned on the backs of her eyeballs for long after the tent went dark.

Now, her ears became more acutely attuned to the sounds around her as he shifted in his sleeping bag. A knee grazed hers, the warmth of his body inspiring a heat that didn't have anything to do with actual core temperature. Outside the wind whistled and howled, but the tent fabric seemed impervious, stretched as tight as her nerves as Weston lay in the inky blackness with her.

"Thank you for coming out here tonight." The words were easier to say in the dark, when she couldn't gauge his expression or see his body language. She'd been confused by both in the past, unable to really read him. "I'm sorry to have ruined your evening with an unplanned trip up the mountain, but I'm grateful."

On his side of the tent, he stilled. Maybe he'd just settled into a comfortable position.

"I got into mountain-rescue work to help people in trouble. But ideally, I'd rather prevent an accident before it happens." When he spoke, his words were so close to her ear, she realized he must be on his side.

Facing her.

She swallowed. Tried to focus on his words and not his nearness as she burrowed deeper into her sleeping bag while attempting not to move too much. She lay on her back, wary of getting any closer to him when she felt vulnerable and, yes, a little scared of what the weather might bring tomorrow. The snowstorm had kicked up into a major event so quickly that it had seriously rattled her confidence on the mountain.

"Yet climbing up here, in the dark, to make sure I got out of there safely? That was above and beyond. I didn't mean for you to take a risk in these deteriorating weather conditions."

Guilt bubbled up in her. She should have tracked the weather more carefully, but the storm had arrived much faster than the forecasters had predicted.

The deep timbre of his voice rumbled through her. "It was better for me to make the climb to help you in person. Not knowing you that well, I didn't want to send you a text that could potentially scare you and have you scrambling around on dangerous terrain."

He'd said as much before, but it didn't make her feel any better about him risking his neck for her sake. What if he'd been injured in the attempt to help her? A whirl of what-ifs spun through her brain. She knew how seemingly innocuous events could lead to major consequences. She remembered all too well the chain of events that had brought her mother to her current state.

"I do have GPS equipment. I could have followed directions," she insisted, not wanting to be the cause of anyone else's trouble. She preferred to be self-sufficient after the years of relying on her mother for care that she'd been incapable of giving. Looking for strength within was her go-to coping mechanism. Besides, the part that really bugged her was that she'd messaged him tonight to find common ground with him for the sake of her investigation.

She'd been fishing for answers, and he'd been completely selfless. The disparity didn't sit well with her.

"With the storm coming in, I knew conditions could change from moment to moment, and that really impacts which way out of the ravine is safest. It was easier to check out the snow and the wind for myself than to give you instructions from my living room." He said it matter-of-factly, like it was an obvious solution.

She bit her tongue for a moment to keep herself from arguing with him since, bottom line, she was grateful. She'd had no idea she'd put herself in such danger tonight.

"Thank you," she said, her gaze wandering over the shape of his shoulder in the darkness as her eyes adjusted to the lack of light. "I feel even worse about you being here, though, considering the way we last parted. I know I'm not high on your list of favorite people."

In the quiet moment that followed, she heard nothing but the wind and the soft plunk of fat snowflakes on the tent roof.

"Your job puts us at odds," he said finally, his words sounding carefully chosen. "And, until tonight, I haven't gotten the chance to know you outside your investigation."

She couldn't help a wry laugh, caused by the guilt and vulnerability of her position. "I don't think tonight is going to raise your opinion of me now that I'm the hapless ranch guest you had to rescue in a snowstorm."

"We're going to be fine, you know," he reassured her, his tone gentle.

Through her sleeping bag, she felt his hand cover her forearm, giving it a comforting squeeze.

Everything inside her went perfectly still. Unbidden, memories of seeing him in the stables with the horses came back to her. She'd observed him unaware before she cornered him in his office to question him. He'd been a wizard with a skittish gelding, calming the animal's restless movements with his steady presence until the horse rested its muzzle on his shoulder and let out a soft sigh.

She'd been mesmerized by Weston then. Just like now.

"You're not worried about how much snow we're getting?" The climb down could be difficult.

"No. And you shouldn't be, either." His hand didn't move away from her forearm.

She felt her heartbeat there, as if her blood pulsed harder through her veins in the place where he touched her. So weird. So…intriguing.

A wave of warmth stole over her, sweet and pleasurable. Tempting and oh, so dangerous. She couldn't afford to let herself be charmed by him. Not when she still had a job to do.

"In that case, I'll try not to think about the storm." What she needed was a distraction. A way to take her mind off the snow. Off the sexy and disarming man lying beside her in the dark. "We could talk about the job I have to do, instead. As long as we're both here."

Still, he didn't move his hand away. That surprised her a little, since she guessed the topic would insert some much-needed frosty distance between them again.

"We could," he said easily, as if he'd really thought it over. "But since you're sharing my roof tonight, and I climbed all this way to save your lovely hide, I think the information is going to cost you."

"Is that so?" She turned her head toward him to see if she could discern his expression. Read his mood. But his face was still in shadow, even if she could see the outline of his broad shoulders.

"Definitely." His voice took on a silky note as he skimmed a touch up her arm to her shoulder.

Her heart rate doubled.

"What are you suggesting?" she asked, with a hint more breathlessness than she would have liked.

"I think a kiss per question would be fair," he told her evenly.

So much for frosty distance. She felt a wave of heat as surely as if someone switched off the snow and turned on a fireplace, and that was the last thing she needed.

"I don't think anyone has tried coercing me into kissing since junior high," she told him drily.

He had the good grace to chuckle. "No coercion intended. Are you sure you can say the same for yourself? Because I won't feel as good about the rescue attempt if you were only hoping to ask me questions about Alonzo Salazar again."

Guilt pinched at her conscience again.

"Fair enough." She turned over in her sleeping bag

to face him, realizing she needed to be on her toes with this man. "Although I'm not sure it speaks well of your kissing skill that you leverage it to discourage me from talking about my c-case."

A shiver rolled through her.

"Are you warm enough?" He slid his coat off his bag and laid it over hers. "This will help."

"Thank you." She fidgeted more in an effort to get comfortable and warm.

"And I have total faith in my kissing skills, for what it's worth. But I took a gamble you were one of those women who won't mix business with pleasure." The last word sounded oddly erotic in the dark. He paused a moment, and then added, "Would you like some help with your bag?"

Weston had thought maybe acknowledging the attraction between them would reroute that busy mind of hers, since she'd been worrying about the weather and feeling guilty for getting them snowed in together.

So his intentions for the flirtatious direction of their conversation had been mostly good. But he had been unable to distract her, and now she sounded chilled.

"I'm trying to find the drawstring so I c-can pull the fabric around my face," she admitted, her shivering more obvious now.

Concerned, he reached for his flashlight.

"Let me," he insisted, clicking the torch on to the

lower setting and pointing it away from them so as not to blind her.

He could see she'd wriggled her sleeping pad off to one side. The material was now bunched between them where it wasn't going to help her stay warm. His coat had fallen off her too, no doubt because she was struggling with the puffy down to find the drawstring.

Cursing himself for getting distracted by his attraction to her, he shifted back to professional mode. Her safety came first.

"I'm going to work fast, okay?" He didn't want to surprise her by manhandling her, but he also didn't want to linger outside his own sleeping bag given that the temperature was probably hovering around fifteen degrees.

She nodded uncertainly, her blue eyes locked on him.

Getting to his knees, he leaned over her to retrieve his coat. Then, he wrapped one arm far enough around her to lift her shoulders. With his other hand, he tugged the corner of the sleeping pad back where it belonged, trying not to notice her soft curves pressed against his chest for one delicious moment. Once he had that smoothed out, he felt along the zipper near her shoulder until he found the drawstring and gave it a tug. The puffy down closed in around her face, leaving just her eyes, nose and highly kissable mouth visible.

Finally, just when the chill was starting to really

bite through his clothes, he laid his coat over her and retreated to his own sleeping bag. He burrowed down fast, zipping up the fabric all the way.

"You must be freezing." Her gaze tracked his movements in a way he welcomed.

That flattering caress of her eyes was the only thing keeping the cold at bay now.

"The temperature has definitely dropped a few degrees," he admitted. "I'm going to wait a minute before I turn off the light." He wanted his arms to warm up first.

"You should take your coat back." She lifted her head a bit as she turned to look at him since her peripheral vision was impeded by the bag. It made her look like a mummy.

"I have a better idea." He didn't want her to give up the coat. "If we share it, we'll both be warmer."

"Okay." She nodded her assent.

"Just until the chill goes away," he assured her, already warmer at the thought of holding her against him.

"Of course." Her breath huffed out in a cloud between them. "I'm not worried about anything…more happening when we're on the verge of icing over."

He suddenly didn't feel one bit icy, but he didn't plan on sharing that with her. Sliding one arm free of his sleeping bag, he snaked it under his coat and wound it around her midsection. He pulled her to him, so her back was to his chest, her rump tucked into his lap.

She made a soft squeak, but she pressed into him, her body plastering itself to his through the layers of down between them. For a moment, he simply held her there, his nose pressed into the back of her hood, his arm brushing the underside of her breasts. She felt good.

Not just because she was warm. April Stephens was soft and pliable in his arms, fitting just right. He slid his other arm under her head for a pillow, figuring she'd keep him warm enough. The protective urge flared along with a lot of other urges he wasn't going to think about.

Much.

"Better?" He spoke the words against her neck through the sleeping bag.

He felt a shiver go through her, but he'd be willing to bet this one was the good kind.

"Much." When she spoke, the vibration of sound hummed along his arm where he held her.

With the snow falling in soft swishes against the canvas tent and a beautiful woman spooned against him, he could almost forget they were still in a potentially dangerous storm. How long had it been since he'd slept with someone in his arms all night? Normally he avoided relationships with those kinds of expectations. He never would have imagined that the financial forensics investigator would be the one who broke his private, unspoken rules about sleepovers. He'd sworn off deeper relationships after he and his brother had fallen for the same woman back in their college days. Brianna had wreaked havoc on him, but she'd done an even worse number on his brother.

"How's your nose?" he asked after a long moment, knowing frostbite could set in fast. "I think that's the only place you have to worry about now."

"Mmm." She made a sleepy sound and snuggled closer to him, her hips rocking in a devastating swivel.

And damned if his body didn't answer the call.

Grinding his teeth against those urges, Weston let go of her long enough to flick off the flashlight. Then, he went back to holding her.

Tomorrow, he'd have to deal with the fallout from coming to her rescue tonight. He wouldn't be able to ignore her anymore after this, wouldn't be able to threaten to call security if she asked too many questions. For that matter, he'd be dodging her queries about his former mentor the whole way down the mountain while he tried to keep her safe through a potentially dangerous descent.

But since tomorrow would come soon enough, he wasn't going to borrow trouble now. For a few hours, at least, he planned to enjoy the hot dreams sure to come from having a sexy woman curled in his arms like she was meant to be there.

Three

Sunlight pried at April's eyes the next morning.

Too early, she thought, for it to be so bright. Her body was exhausted. And hot.

Pulling herself from layers of sleep, she struggled to figure out why she'd be so warm. Her limbs were pinned by a heavy weight on one side. Her nose was buried against…a man?

Memories of the night before returned in a moment as blinding as the sun streaming across one side of her face. The avalanche threat. The trudge through deep snow only to make camp with Weston. Falling asleep in his arms.

Which was a spot she'd clearly enjoyed, based on the way she was wrapped around him now like a second skin. How had her sleeping bag unzipped enough to allow so much proximity? She had one arm threaded under his to splay across his strong back. One thigh tucked between his. Her cheek and nose were pressed tight to his chest, where his heartbeat slugged. The fabric of the thermal shirt he wore hugged every inch of him as tightly as she did.

But the point of all the heat she felt was focused in the cradle of her hips, where the most intriguing part of his anatomy stirred.

Her breath caught in a strangled gasp as she scrambled back.

Weston let go of her immediately, making her realize he'd been awake the whole time. Which only added to her flustered state.

"Good morning." His voice was rough from sleep, his tone polite and reasonable, though she detected a hint of mild amusement.

"Is it?" she asked, confused to note her covers twisted around one knee while the rest of her remained under the warmth of his heavy coat.

Her gaze went to his body, where she caught a glimpse of his powerful legs and narrow hips before he shifted his own sleeping bag over him like a blanket.

"We're still here," he reminded her. "Whole and warm, ready for another day. I'd call that good news after the weather conditions we faced last night."

Belatedly, she noticed the snowdrift on one side of the tent was almost halfway up the canvas wall.

No doubt that had helped insulate them against the cold, along with the natural body heat they'd gained by wrapping themselves around each other.

"I don't know how my sleeping bag unzipped." She couldn't help but raise the issue, since it embarrassed her to think she'd helped herself to Weston's body during the night.

She liked to think she had a stronger-than-average sense of personal space. Healthy boundaries. And while she'd been fine with pressing together through the fabric of two down barriers when they'd been trying to go to sleep, she felt completely undone at the idea of waking up with her leg between his thighs.

Lifting her gaze to his face, she was stunned all over again to notice how little space still separated them. During the night, at least, it had been dark enough that she couldn't see his perceptive hazel gaze on her.

"You probably did that in your sleep." He was a kind man to give her a face-saving excuse for why she was attached to him like a barnacle this morning. "I woke up a couple of hours into the storm and realized I was burning up, so I unzipped my sleeping bag and used it like a blanket."

"Hmm." She was all too aware of how hot things had gotten during the coldest night she'd ever spent outdoors.

Talking about it wasn't going to make her any less flustered.

If anything, her body still tingled with awareness

everywhere she'd touched him. She couldn't remember the last time she'd felt so alive, like every nerve ending had been awakened at the hands of this man. Why did he have to be someone so important to her investigation? For a moment, she wondered what might have happened between them if she didn't have that professional duty holding her back.

Well, that and the fact that Weston was anxious for her to take her questions and leave Mesa Falls Ranch. She couldn't do that until she'd tracked down answers, and she'd do well to remember that barrier between them since she'd been so quick to tear down the physical ones. Her subconscious obviously wanted him, even if the rest of her knew that was a very bad idea. She needed this job. The order, the respectability had saved her in so many ways. Without it? Hell, she couldn't even consider risking her job for anyone.

"How do you feel this morning, April?" he asked, jarring her from her worries. "Are you ready to try the descent now that the snow has stopped?"

Sunlight beckoned.

And so did the chance to resurrect boundaries with the compelling man next to her.

She nodded, already mentally ticking through today's to-do list to keep herself from thinking about Weston. "I can have my gear packed in five minutes."

Her five-minute prediction turned out to be optimistic. April hadn't counted on how much the deep snow would hamper her efforts, or how much her mother's phone calls would distract her.

She'd ignored the first two times the notifications chimed as she laced up her boots and loaded her backpack. But by the third time the chime sounded as they began the descent, she was too worried not to pick up.

Weston had insisted on walking in front of her to check the soundness of the snow. He'd given himself the much harder job in the process, since his powerful stride cleared a path for her. Even so, the deep, fluffy powder was exhausting to wade through.

"Mom?" she answered once she fished the device from her pocket, knowing she needed to make this brief. For her own safety, she had to focus on what she was doing. "Is anything wrong? I'm on the mountain, so it's not the best time—"

"I just wanted you to know that I've fired the cleaning service." Breathing heavily, her mother sounded tearful.

Anxiety spiked, but April tried not to let it explode into full-blown panic. The cleaners were expensive because they specialized in helping people like Holly Stephens. April had hired them, not her mom, so she didn't think they could be fired so easily.

"I'm sorry they've upset you." She dragged in a long breath of the cleansing cold, preparing to smooth things over with the company. "Can I speak to Emily and maybe I can get things sorted out?"

"It's too late for that!" Her mother's voice rose an

octave. "I tried calling you before it came to that, but you were too busy to help."

April swallowed convulsively. She loved her mom, but she hated this stress. It was difficult enough when she was in the same town as her mother, but now, many miles from her Denver home, there was nothing she could do to fix things.

"I'm sorry, Mom." She kept her voice low, hoping Weston couldn't hear all of this. Even though he wore a fleece headband around his ears today instead of a balaclava, she wasn't banking on it. "I'm in Montana right now, hiking through snow and hazardous conditions or I would come over—"

"It's no problem." Her mother cut her off, a new curtness in her voice. "I just wanted you to know so you didn't harass me about the cleaning company anymore. Emily wanted me to throw out one of the brand-new bolts of fabric. Have you ever heard of such waste?"

With some murmured words of sympathy, April was able to extricate herself from the call a few moments later, but the worry remained. Keeping her mother safe required more time and money every year, sacrifices April would gladly make if it truly helped. But when her mom resisted more and more frequently, it made her efforts feel futile.

"Everything okay?" Weston called back over his broad shoulder, lifting his goggles to look at her.

For a moment, as she saw the concern in his expression and heard it in his voice, she allowed herself to wonder what it would be like to have someone like that in her life. Someone who cared about her daily trials. Someone to share the burden with.

It was a crazy, foolish thought for someone like Weston to inspire, since he was decidedly off-limits as a key to her investigation. Besides, the life of a wealthy and influential rancher was a world apart from the one she lived.

"Everything's fine," she lied, needing to resurrect some mental and emotional boundaries with the man she'd spent a memorable night with.

"Didn't sound fine." He slowed his pace so she could catch up with him, his hazel gaze tracking her, sliding right past those boundaries she needed. But perhaps he read her reticence in her eyes, because he changed topics as she neared him. "Are you warm enough? Am I going too fast?"

Grateful for the reprieve from talking about her mom and even more grateful to seize on the topic of climbing, which had always been her favorite escape from her home life, she launched into questions about the terrain. How he read the snow, how he could tell what kind of surface was beneath it, what to look for when gauging avalanche conditions.

All things she was interested in. All much safer topics than her mom. If only she could distract herself from her attraction to him as easily.

It didn't take an expert in body language to read April's cues.

Weston had seen the guardedness in her expression after her tense phone call, so he'd given her an out and she'd grabbed it like a lifeline. At first, he'd thought she was just trying to distract him from asking questions, but her curiosity about the Bitterroot Mountains and his rescue work revealed a dedicated climber's knowledge. He found himself enjoying the long trudge down to his truck, a trip that took far longer than it should have given the depth of the snow. Besides, he knew she'd been exhausted the night before. He didn't want her to deplete her energy completely.

Plus, he was glad to forge a connection on another level after the awkward way she'd awoken in his arms that morning. He didn't know who'd made the first move to initiate the contact, but he'd never forget the feel of her soft and warm in his arms. She didn't know that he'd emerged from sleep before her, or that he'd found his hand tantalizingly affixed to her breast. Thank goodness she didn't know. Breaking that contact had been what had awoken her. Those sensory memories had tormented him all day long.

Now, as they paused for a water break and a shared protein bar, he found himself wanting to know more about her. About what caused those shadows in her eyes after the call from her mother. He understood something about painful family relationships. And while he wasn't in the habit of revealing details of his personal life, he couldn't help but think that a shared experience might help her, if only to remind this strong, capable woman that she wasn't alone.

After capping the water, they renewed their trek. The path widened and the incline decreased, making the walking easier. She stayed close to him, her cheeks flushed pink from the exercise, but she kept pace without a problem. He'd done this descent hundreds of times himself, so it was simple enough to focus on her. The conditions were solid here even with the foot of fresh powder. A winter wonderland glittered all around them, dazzling white from the intense sun.

"I won't ask you about your family," he began, hoping to put her at ease. "But I can tell you that living far from mine has improved my relationship with them." Which still wasn't saying much, considering they hardly spoke. But it was better than the hurtful exchanges they'd had all too often when he lived on the family's ranch.

"You're fortunate you have that option," she said tightly, breath huffing in the cold air.

"I realize that. I'm often reminded how lucky I am to have a brother who has never made a misstep in his life at the helm of our family's ranch." Weston wasn't exactly bitter. It was tough to hold a grudge against Miles when he'd never done a damned thing wrong. "But I found it frustrating to continually fall short of my parents' expectations for me."

"You're the black sheep?" She sounded surprised.

"That's putting it kindly." On second thought, the tension in his shoulders just thinking about the Rivera family made him realize how much he didn't care to unearth old pains, even for her benefit. "But it did help to put some physical distance between me and them. Do you have siblings?"

"No. Just me." She was quiet for so long he nearly replied, but then she continued. "And my mother isn't someone I can leave alone for long. She has a hoarding disorder, in addition to some other issues that aren't as obvious or well managed, and I worry about her safety when I'm not with her."

"That sounds stressful." He didn't know what he'd been expecting, but it hadn't been that. "Is she getting treatment?"

"Not as much as I would like." April's boots trudged a soft rhythm beside his, and he took in how she tucked her thumbs under the straps of her backpack as she redistributed the weight on her shoulders. "The condition was only recently reclassified as a distinct mental health issue, and I feel like her current doctor isn't doing all she can to help with my mother's specific problems."

"Is your father around to help?" Weston realized he was on more precarious terrain in the conversation than they were on the mountainside as the landscape evened out a bit more. He hadn't meant to pry.

"No. They divorced when I was in my teens, after the house started getting out of control with

Mom's purchases." She gave an awkward shrug as they ducked into a thicket of trees. "I'm the only one Mom has."

"That's a lot for you. For any one person." It also said a hell of a lot about the burdens she carried. No wonder she was a fearless climber. Real life had thrown her plenty of other obstacles.

"There are more and more resources out there. Even if I can't get as much aid from her doctor as I would like, at least we have access to more programs as social awareness of the condition grows." She glanced his way just as his all-terrain vehicle, completely covered in a mound of snow, finally came into view at the trailhead. "Is that yours?"

"Yes." He offered her a smile, grateful to be close to home again but regretting not getting to learn more about her while she'd been sharing her story with him. "We're almost home free."

Reaching the vehicle, they worked side by side to brush off the worst of the snow. He noticed April gave herself completely to the task; apparently she was done talking for the day. While he understood that urge to shut down about family, he couldn't help but ask one more question.

"What set you on your career path? Financial forensics seems fairly specialized." Once he could open a door of his ATV freely, he withdrew a compact snow shovel and dug around the wheels, just enough to get them going.

They'd be fine once the ATV was in motion, but

he needed some space around it to gain traction and momentum first.

She smoothed her glove along the top of a tire, swiping off the snow with her hand since there was only one shovel. "I received an accounting degree but worked for a PI in college to make some extra cash. I sat on stakeouts, followed cheaters, took some pictures…just legwork. Being around his office helped me to see my path."

Standing up straight, Weston moved to the last tire as his brain shuffled through the new information.

"Now you follow money instead of people." He could see where the order of finances would appeal to someone who grew up the way she'd described.

"People can try to create a smokescreen with their finances, but in the end, the numbers don't lie."

Her assessment of her job stuck with him as he loaded their packs in the vehicle. He'd heard the note of pride in her voice. It was obvious she gained professional satisfaction from succeeding at her work. Which only underscored his certainty that she wouldn't let this case go.

Opening the passenger-side door for her, he asked, "Are you ready to return to civilization?"

"Yes, please." She pulled off her hat and goggles, her blue eyes a clear, deep sea as she peered up at him.

Memories of waking up to her in his arms returned. The awareness of her hadn't retreated, even with the reminder that her work was going to be a thorn in his side.

"And you're still staying at the main lodge?" He knew for a fact she hadn't checked out. But he was curious what she'd say about her plans moving forward. As much as he resented her investigation, her work was being financed by Devon Salazar, Alonzo's son. So Weston preferred not to ask her to leave outright.

Ideally, she would give up on her own without anyone at Mesa Falls having to cross swords with the Salazar heirs.

"I am." She stepped into the ATV. "I'll be at Mesa Falls Ranch until I find the answers I need."

Grinding his teeth, he closed her door, then slid into the driver's seat and fired up the engine, trying to figure out what that meant for him.

He really should be keeping track of her progress on the investigation since he had a vested interest in keeping his former mentor out of the public eye. If April uncovered Alonzo's secrets—and he was beginning to think she wouldn't give up until she did just that—Weston needed to be there for damage control. Or to spin the story more favorably.

Just the thought of it made his shoulders tense up again.

He debated his next move as he drove them down the mountain. He passed his house, pointing it out to April on the way to the main lodge. By the time he arrived at her accommodations and switched off the engine, he knew he couldn't return to his old way of dealing with her by ignoring her. There was no denying they'd forged some kind of connection on that mountain. If anything, he was already thinking about what it would be like to wake up next to her again. In a much warmer bed.

Mind made up, and intrigued by the prospect of seeing her again, he opened his door and retrieved her backpack before coming around to assist her. The snow wasn't as deep here, telling him the storm hadn't been nearly as bad in the valley as it had been on the peaks.

"I can't thank you enough for coming to my aid last night, Weston," she said as she took his hand and allowed him to help her from the low vehicle.

"You can if you have dinner with me tonight." He liked the plan even more when he saw a momentary flash of feminine interest in her eyes.

Awareness.

The expression was fleeting, though, quickly replaced by a nervous nibble on her lip as she reached for her bag.

"I'm not sure that's a good idea, since my investigation is sure to put us at odds again." She hugged her backpack closer.

Did she feel like she needed a barrier with him? The idea gave him pause. He sure as hell didn't want to make her nervous.

"I understand." He wouldn't pressure her. She'd had an exhausting couple of days, made more stressful by whatever crisis was happening at home. "But you know where to find me, and I promise no more threatening to have security cart you off if you want to talk."

A small smile played around her lips at the reminder of their previous meeting.

"Even if I ask nosy questions?"

"I think we've passed that point in our relationship after last night." He wasn't going to pretend something significant hadn't happened up there. "You have a job to do, and I respect that."

That didn't mean he had to like it.

"And you still want to have dinner?" she clarified, her professional mind clearly at work on the problem.

Sensing victory, he was surprised at the rush of pleasure he felt at the idea of spending an evening with her. She'd gotten under his skin fast.

"I do." He relished the idea of seeing her relaxed by candlelight. Last night had been too anxiety-filled for both of them. "We deserve to toast our success in weathering the storm."

Just thinking about something happening to her made his gut go cold again.

"In that case, I will have dinner with you, Weston." She smiled, and he caught a glimpse of another side of her that he hadn't seen before. It wasn't deliberately flirtatious, but it was definitely aware.

A blast of heated attraction banished the chill of a moment prior, and he couldn't wait for tonight.

Four

Revising her case leads in one of the ranch's public lounges that afternoon, April should have been exhausted from the night spent on the mountain and the climb down afterward. Instead, she felt a renewed energy for solving her case as she sipped her chilled seltzer with a twist of lime and scrolled through notes on her tablet. The lounge was quiet at this hour, with most of the guests engaged in outdoor activities in the waning daylight. A country love song twanged through the speaker system while a fire crackled in the stone hearth close to April's quiet booth table. She'd been here for over an hour, trying not to think too much about her upcoming date with Weston.

An impossible task, and no doubt the reason behind her feeling of restless energy. Her thoughts kept returning to their time together. And the promise of seeing him again for dinner. She wanted to believe that she'd agreed to the date to further her investigation. To see if she could learn more about Alonzo Salazar while she tried to unravel the mystery of Weston's loyalty to the man.

But she knew that her attraction to Weston played into the decision as much as—or more than—anything. If it had been purely physical, maybe she could have ignored the draw of the man. But he'd risked his own neck in a snowstorm to make sure she was safe. He'd helped her even though he'd been doing his damnedest to stay away. How could she not be intrigued and enticed?

With an effort, she pulled her thoughts away from Weston to focus on her leads. She set her glass of water on the cork coaster while she scanned an online forum devoted to Hollywood. There was an active discussion of actress Tabitha Barnes's recent revelation that Alonzo Salazar was the man behind the pseudonym A. J. Sorensen, the author of the book *Hollywood Newlyweds*. A book that had destroyed Tabitha's family. For maximum impact and press exposure, she'd made the announcement at a celebrity-studded gala that had taken place at Mesa Falls Ranch—the kickoff event for the ranch's expansion from private corporate retreat to a more public luxury ranch destination. April had been on-site then for the start of her investigation into Alonzo Salazar's finances, and

the revelation that her target was the reclusive author
had changed the trajectory of her case significantly.
Alonzo's son Devon Salazar had hired her firm to find
out where his father's money had disappeared, and
the case had gotten decidedly thornier after Tabitha
Barnes's big reveal.

"Ms. Stephens?" A feminine voice made her look
up.

An auburn-haired young woman dressed in the
khakis and white sweater that marked her as a ranch
employee hovered near her elbow. Her gold name
tag read Nicole.

"Yes?" She was surprised the staffer knew her
name. Momentary panic for her mother bubbled
though her. Had something gone wrong back home?

"I'm sorry to interrupt." The woman glanced over
her shoulder, as if to make sure no one would over-
hear them, eyes darting swiftly around the lounge
before she lowered her voice. "I've contacted your
office a couple of times to try to share some information. For your investigation?"

Puzzled, April shuffled the pieces in her mind,
realizing there was no crisis at home. How had a
ranch worker come to learn about her case? Turning
off her tablet screen without breaking eye contact,
April gestured toward the seat across from her, inviting the woman to sit down.

"I never received that message." She wondered
why. Had her office not forwarded the information?

Or was the woman lying? "But you're welcome to join me."

She'd take any lead she could get at this point. Alonzo Salazar had employed a nominee service through a law office that allowed him to be publicly anonymous, financially speaking. Although the service should have expired after his death, it was possible he'd paid for it in advance, since the law office hadn't broken their silence yet on where his funds from the book had gone.

The young woman hesitated. "The staff aren't supposed to dine in here, but maybe if I just sit for a moment."

She lowered herself into the booth, still glancing around the mostly empty lounge.

"Why don't you start by telling me your name?" April prodded, used to reluctant parties giving her information in small doses. People were often worried about being implicated in a crime when money was being used in questionable ways.

"Nicole… Smith." The smallest hesitation before giving the common surname told April it was most likely false. The woman toyed with the name tag on her sweater for a moment before slipping it off. "I've only worked here since the start of the New Year. I came to Mesa Falls Ranch after seeing the gala on the news."

"The ranch really put itself on the map after that." April smiled warmly to encourage confidences. "I haven't seen any celebrities here this week, unfortunately."

Nicole nodded quickly, speaking in a rush. "I was most interested in what Tabitha Barnes said about the real identity of the guy who wrote *Hollywood Newlyweds*."

"And how did you find out I'm interested in that too?" April pressed, since Nicole seemed ready to get down to business with this discussion.

"I tried getting in touch with Devon Salazar once I learned Alonzo's name." Nicole spun the gold name tag on the table. "And after a few phone calls, he suggested I contact you."

Interesting. That told April she was both persistent and—possibly—had something worthwhile to share.

"Did you do that before or after you took a job here?"

Nicole's gaze flicked up to hers. Held. "Right around the same time. It was easy getting hired on here with so many new job openings after the gala."

The buzzing in April's ears told her she was getting closer to answers. Clearly Nicole was serious about digging deeper into Alonzo's mysterious past.

"You've got my full attention." April forced herself to stay perfectly still, keeping her body language relaxed even though she was on the edge of her proverbial seat. "What information were you hoping to share with me?"

Nicole squared her shoulders. Leaning closer, she lowered her voice even more.

"I might know where Alonzo's money has been going," she confided, her red hair spilling onto the table as it fell forward.

April's pulse sped at the possible lead.

Finally.

She waited until Nicole spoke again. "I think he's been financing the education and upbringing of my thirteen-year-old nephew."

Nicole Cruz had taken a calculated risk sharing her family's secrets with a virtual stranger.

But she was running out of resources and needed help fast to continue her quest for the truth. Right now, it seemed like financial forensics expert April Stephens was her best hope of solving the mystery of the paternity of Nicole's sister's son.

When Lana died of an aneurysm six months ago, her secrets had died with her. Including the identity of Matthew's father. Even though a mysterious benefactor had pitched in to pay for the boy's private schooling—a boarding school with the excellent resources a bright and promising autistic preteen required to thrive—that didn't cover all the expenses associated with Matthew's care. Not that Nicole regretted the sacrifices she'd made for him. Not for an instant. She wouldn't trade the joys of having Mattie in her life for anything. But now that Lana was gone, Nicole wasn't inclined to let the boy's father off the hook for his responsibility the way her sister had. Matthew deserved his father's support—financially, if nothing else.

And her only lead to his father?

Alonzo Salazar.

"What evidence do you have to support the theory?" April asked, the picture of elegant composure in her navy blue blazer and pale blue cashmere sweater underneath it.

With her perfect blond curls spiraling around her shoulders, the financial forensics investigator stood out from the other ranch guests in their expensive cowboy boots and brand-new Stetsons. April Stephens looked like the kind of woman who didn't allow herself to get rattled. Her understated makeup was pretty without being showy. Everything about her announced that she was smart and efficient.

Or maybe that was wishful thinking. Nicole needed a lifeline if she was going to solve the question of who Matthew's father was before the boy's spring break. Once Mattie returned to their San Jose home next month, Nicole needed to be back in California. Her spur-of-the-moment ranch job would come to an end, and with it, her best chance of getting close to the truth. For now, she tried to share enough details with April to entice her to follow the story, but she wasn't willing to give her real name yet. Or Lana's, for that matter.

"My sister—Matthew's mother—never named the boy's father before she passed away last fall. But toward the end, she told me not to worry about Matthew because his education was being paid for. When I pressed her for details, because she was—" She had to stop her story suddenly, the memory of her sister's last moments causing a shock of a pain so sharp it took her breath away.

She blinked, tried to see past the hurt, and the ache only sharpened. To her mortification, tears welled.

"Let me get you a drink." April rushed out of the booth and hurried to the bar, demanding a water from the older guy who was reorganizing the beer glasses.

Nicole was grateful for the reprieve. She took the moment to surreptitiously steal the linen napkin from an unused place setting so she could dab at her eyes. By the time April returned, she had herself under control again.

"My apologies," she managed between sips of the water April gave her. "And thank you for this."

"Of course. I'm so sorry for the loss of your sister." The words sounded heartfelt, and Nicole was grateful for them.

She'd spent so much time reeling from all the life changes since Lana's death that she hadn't really grieved. That was, she grieved all the time, since losing Lana was like losing a limb. But she hadn't ever given in to the need to weep over the unfairness of it all. Maybe she feared once she started crying, she wouldn't stop.

Whatever the reason, she couldn't afford to take that time now. Not when she was finally sitting across from someone who might be able to help her secure a better, more stable future for Matthew.

"Thank you." Sliding the cut-crystal glass to one side, she met April's clear blue gaze. "Shortly before she passed, my sister made a mention of A. J. Sorensen providing for her son. At the time, I thought she was delirious or that I hadn't understood her properly."

In truth, her sister had simply tapped the cover of the book *Hollywood Newlyweds* since it had been on the nightstand of her hospital room. So Nicole thought she hadn't really known what she was pointing at.

"What made you change your mind?" April prodded at the same moment that Nicole's shift supervisor poked her head into the bar, her disapproving glare falling on Nicole.

She needed to get back to work. Her break from her desk job in guest services had ended five minutes ago. And technically, she wasn't supposed to spend her break in the hospitality areas. So she talked fast.

"When Tabitha Barnes made her announcement that A. J. Sorensen was Alonzo, the pieces fell into place, since we knew him." She needed to get back to work, and she slid out of the booth, taking her name tag with her. "Look, I can't talk now, but tomorrow is my day off. I can meet you."

Frowning, April covered Nicole's hand with hers.

"Are you suggesting that Alonzo fathered your sister's son?"

"I seriously doubt it," she told her honestly, passing over a scrap of paper with her phone number scribbled on it. "She was only twenty-one at the time, and Alonzo was much older." Nicole had never gotten any hint that Matthew had been conceived under circumstances like that, and Lana had always seemed to like Alonzo well enough from what little they'd seen of him. But she didn't treat him like the father of her child.

April shifted in her seat as if she was prepared to follow her. "Nicole, just one more thing—"

"Tomorrow, okay?" She hoped she hadn't made a mistake by confiding in April Stephens. The woman was being employed by Alonzo's son, after all. What if April decided it was in the Salazar family's best interests to cut off support to Matthew altogether? "I can't afford to lose this job."

She'd lost too much already.

Every time April picked up her phone to cancel her date with Weston, she ended up setting it back down again.

Which was why she ended up dressed and ready for an evening with him even though she was far too flustered about her case to enjoy herself. Of course, an evening spent with him wasn't *supposed* to be self-indulgent. She'd made the commitment to have dinner with Weston so she could learn something useful to help along her investigation. Now, she was distracted by leads she wanted to follow up on when the knock sounded on the door to her suite promptly at 7:00 p.m.

Swallowing hard, she forced herself to stand perfectly still in the middle of the living area floor for a moment while she collected her thoughts. She'd dressed on autopilot, settling on the only cocktail dress she'd brought on the trip. Long-sleeved and silky, the plum-colored sheath was plain except for the slashes in the crepe sleeves and the keyhole slit in the bodice underneath an otherwise high neck. Odd how those small hints of skin seemed so provocative in an otherwise conservative dress, but maybe it was just her thoughts about Weston that made her so self-aware tonight.

Get it together.

She couldn't afford to let her guard drop around him. Especially not if he was protecting a man who harbored as many secrets as Alonzo Salazar. Anger simmered at the possibility that Salazar had fathered a child without publicly acknowledging him as his son. Frustration fueled her steps as she charged toward the door to answer it. To confront Weston.

Yanking open the door faster than she'd intended, she realized she hadn't been prepared for the sight of him in evening attire. He was dressed head to toe in black, his jacket and silk shirt matching his polished boots. The lack of tie and the open top button on his shirt were the only casual notes.

"You look beautiful." He stepped into the suite and greeted her with a kiss on the cheek, so quick and perfunctory she might have written it off as mere politeness on his part if her skin didn't tingle there long afterward, the hint of teakwood aftershave teasing her nose.

"Thank you." She reached for her coat on the elk-horn stand near the door, but he beat her to it, his hand covering hers for a moment before he took over the task.

"Allow me." He slipped the black wool coat around her shoulders, gently sliding her hair out from under the fabric once he'd settled it there. His hands lingered on her shoulders briefly.

Squeezing slightly before letting her go.

Her belly tightened in response as he stepped around her to hold the door for her. Desire and defensiveness warred inside her as she thought about how to survive the evening with her self-respect intact. She couldn't give in to the temptation of Weston's natural charisma. Couldn't let her thoughts linger on what it had been like to wake up in his arms this morning.

She would need to be relentless in her quest for answers. She refused to let him off the hook if he was protecting Alonzo Salazar.

Biding her time, she simply followed Weston into the elevator and down to the lobby of the main guest lodge. Steeling herself to his charm, she allowed him to lead her out into the cold Montana evening. They crossed a carefully swept path to one of the older ranch buildings. Graying and weathered, the small barn had been renovated with a large stone patio around it that led down to a skating pond. A few couples were taking advantage of the skating area now, lit by three powerful outdoor lights shining down on the shiny surface of the ice. Country music filled the air from invisible speakers, giving the night a festive feel.

April had seen bigger events take place out here in the time she'd been a guest at Mesa Falls, but she'd never been inside the building where Weston led her now. Only a few lights twinkled from the renovated barn, but the scent of roasted meat and sweet spices hung in the air as he opened a side door.

Stepping onto a thick braided wool rug, April wiped the snow from the high heels she'd worn, the thick ribbons around her ankles drooping slightly. A huge fire burned in a brick hearth along one wall where a single table held place settings for two. No music played indoors, but she could still hear the steel guitars from outside on the pond.

"Your table awaits," Weston said as he slid her coat from her shoulders, his knuckles grazing her skin through the slashes in the crepe sleeves of her dress.

The shiver that went through her didn't have anything to do with the cold.

But it was a welcome reminder that she needed to confront him. He'd told her he wasn't going to try ignoring her questions any longer. Hadn't he assured her he wasn't going to threaten to ask security to remove her from the ranch again?

So as soon as he slid her chair under the table and seated himself across from her, she came quickly to the point.

"I've had a break in the case, Weston." She met his hazel gaze in the flickering candlelight of a single white taper, trying not to wish that their date could have been for fun. For romantic reasons. She stuffed down those thoughts to focus on what she'd learned. "A new lead about where Alonzo's money has been going."

Five

Damn. He hadn't wanted to talk business tonight. Not when April looked the way she did, a hot flame in deep purple silk, her beautiful body draped in crepe with peeks of skin that tantalized the hell out of him.

Regret settled over him like ashes on the wind, slowly stifling the hunger for her so he could concentrate on her words.

"Care to share?" he prompted her when she didn't seem inclined to continue.

He had no idea what his mentor had done with his money, and frankly, he hadn't thought it was any of his business. But after Tabitha Barnes's stunt at the kickoff gala for Mesa Falls Ranch, revealing Alonzo as the author of a Hollywood tell-all, Weston had gotten a bad feeling about the guy's secrets. Alonzo Salazar had known too much about all of the owners of the ranch. Could those secrets come back to hurt them now?

Weston needed to protect their business and, yes, their secrets. They had too much to lose if all the nuances of their past came to light. So he was going to have to tread carefully with April and not get distracted by the attraction between them. His gaze slid briefly to the narrow gap in the fabric between her breasts, her pale skin warmed to burnished bronze by the firelight.

"I spoke to a young woman who believes he's paying for the schooling of her thirteen-year-old nephew." April's words cut through his desire. "A motherless child whose paternity is in question."

Thirteen years old?

Weston didn't need a reminder of the upheaval that had been going on in his life then. Upheaval that Alonzo had been a part of. A foreboding chill raced up his spine.

"What child?" Weston needed more facts before he jumped to conclusions. "You think Alonzo had other offspring he never acknowledged?"

"It's possible. Although the mother was much younger than him." Her lips compressed into a line before April spoke again. "And as you know, Alonzo was working at the Dowdon School fourteen years ago when the child would have been conceived."

The school Weston had attended with all five other owners of Mesa Falls Ranch. April knew about that connection. Alonzo had been their class adviser.

The foreboding grew colder. Sharper. Especially since it was far more likely the father was someone who had been closer to the girl's age. Like Weston would have been at the time, or any of his classmates.

"Who? Who's the mother?"

The Dowdon School hadn't been coed at the time. Very few girls crossed their paths except on carefully chaperoned outings where they attended dances at one of the other schools or went on a trail ride. His thoughts were racing, a cold sweat popping along his forehead at the memory of the worst trail ride of his life. Had one of his friends fathered a child without knowing?

Hell. Had he? He'd been careful, but those had been the roughest years of his life.

"I'm still investigating that." April's brow furrowed in frustration. "I have to assume the woman I spoke to gave me a fake name—Nicole Smith. She said the boy's name is Matthew, but she didn't give me her sister's name. Matthew's mother."

"Nicole Smith? I don't know her."

April unlatched a satin evening purse she'd laid on the chair beside her and withdrew her phone. Powering up the screen, she slid the device across the table to him before she spoke again. "This is her as an adult." She showed him a grainy employee ID photo from the ranch. "I haven't obtained a photo from when she was a teen, let alone found a photo of the sister. If there is one."

"You're suggesting she could be the mother herself?" he asked, looking at the photo again but still coming up blank.

"It's possible. She said her sister was twenty-one at the time, whereas she herself would have only been fifteen, assuming her age is correct on her employee application."

"Twenty-one?" he mused aloud, his brain trying to align the facts she'd shared. "Alonzo would have been in his mid-forties."

April arched a pale eyebrow at him before tucking her phone back in her purse. He waved off the server who'd arrived at their table with a water pitcher and wine that Weston had selected ahead of time. He took over the serving duties, pouring drinks for both of them so they could continue their discussion privately.

Faced with assumptions about Alonzo she'd left unspoken, Weston realized he might need to break his longtime silence on that nightmare summer fourteen years ago. He couldn't stay silent and let his old mentor's reputation go up in flames. Gut sinking, he took a deep breath and met April's blue gaze across the table.

"I realize that Alonzo made a questionable decision to write that book in the first place. That doesn't make him categorically a bad person." Weston took a sip of the pinot noir he'd chosen to pair with their elk medallions. Not that he would be able to enjoy the meal or his compelling companion if he couldn't wind up this discussion fast.

"He wasn't a faithful romantic partner to any of the women in his life, either," April noted drily before she sampled her own wine. "He didn't believe in marriage and insisted on being single all his life despite fathering Marcus and Devon with women on opposite coasts."

"Point taken. But maybe the reason he insisted on not marrying was because he had enough self-awareness to realize he would make a terrible husband." Weston had spent a considerable amount of time with the guy in the years before his death, because Alonzo liked the peaceful solitude of the ranch. "But you haven't spoken to my aunt Fallon, who dated him later in life, and she might have a different perspective to offer."

Their server returned, discreetly sliding a sampler platter of the chef's specialties onto the table between them. The scents of cured trout and bison short ribs wafted from the dish. The fireplace warmed them on one side of their table, while the view of the skating pond beckoned from a tall window on the other. Weston's gaze remained on April, however. She drew his attention again and again. Not just because she was lovely, but because of *her*.

He wanted to know more about what made this fascinating woman tick, and he regretted having to spend their time together rehashing a past he'd rather forget. What would she think of him if she discovered his role in that long-ago summer?

April waited until the server departed. "I would like very much to speak to your aunt. I made the trip to Kalispell to speak to her before the holidays, but she was out of town."

"You may think I tipped her off that you were coming, but I promise you that I did no such thing." He had been actively avoiding April's questions then, but he hadn't done anything else to thwart her case. "Anyway, I don't believe that Alonzo fathered a child with a woman half his age during the years he spent at Dowdon, as I'm sure DNA results will attest."

April's small frown plumped her lower lip in a way that had him wanting a taste of her. He suppressed the hunger by busying himself with serving her from the sampler platter. He slid some of the tasting selections toward her before filling his own appetizer plate.

"I suppose you're right. We could discount Alonzo easily enough if one of his sons will participate in a DNA test." She cut her food into precise portions. Neat. Orderly. "So, assuming he's not the father, why do you think he would pay for this particular child's education after taking pains to hide the money trail?"

"Maybe he felt a responsibility toward one of the child's parents. It's far more likely that the father of the child was a Dowdon student."

"Possibly one of your classmates?" She hesitated,

her fork hovering in midair. "One of the ranch's co-owners?"

"No." He dismissed the idea now that he'd had more time to think about it, his head crowding with old memories of his friends. They weren't the most outwardly likable group of guys he'd ever known, but he trusted them. They were good men. Honorable men. "If Alonzo knew that one of the Mesa Falls Ranch owners had that kind of responsibility, he wouldn't have rested until we owned up to it. He would never settle for secretly financing a kid's education himself."

"Why not?" April leaned closer, a single blond curl falling forward to rest on her forearm near her water glass. "That is, how can you be so sure of his character?"

He weighed his responses, knowing he took a risk trusting her with the story that would help her better understand Alonzo. What if she turned her focus from Salazar to the ranch owners, who all carried a burden of guilt for that long-ago summer? But he'd witnessed April's work in her investigation, and he respected her methods. He'd rather take his chances with her than with the tabloid media that had been swarming the ranch ever since Tabitha Barnes's revelation about Alonzo.

"Because Alonzo Salazar was a good mentor to me at the darkest time in my life."

April knew that Weston's words were heartfelt. She could see the sincerity in his hazel eyes. Did that mean he was closer to sharing the truth with her? Part of her regretted having to pry into his personal life for her case, especially when she'd grown to like him. Would he have ever shared anything personal about himself otherwise, she wondered.

"He was your class adviser at school." She'd learned that much, but it didn't account for the bond between them. "But you obviously maintained a relationship with him long afterward."

Nodding, Weston straightened in his chair, his food hardly touched even though everything was excellent. She took another bite of the bison short ribs, wishing she could simply enjoy this feast for the senses. The food and wine. The seductively appealing man across from her.

"We all did," Weston admitted, seeming to choose his words carefully. "And for you to understand why, I'm going to share a story with you that I need you to keep in confidence."

She felt like she was on the precipice of a key break in her work—in an even bigger way than she'd felt this afternoon with Nicole Smith. Once pieces of a puzzle began to fall in place, the final picture always seemed to come into focus with startling speed.

"You have my word." She understood there were trade-offs to obtaining information.

They were all alone in the renovated barn space. The chef and waitstaff were in the kitchen while Weston and April finished the appetizer course. Not that she could bring herself to eat at the moment; she was too riveted by what Weston had to say.

He nodded, appearing satisfied with her response. "Fourteen years ago, when I was a sophomore at Dowdon, a group of us went horseback riding deep in the Ventana Wilderness close to the school in Southern California." Pausing, he drained the rest of his wine and then set the glass aside. "There were seven of us. All of the owners of Mesa Falls Ranch, plus one other student. Only six of us returned."

A chill tripped over her at his words. Not just because of the implication, but also because of the shuttered look in his eyes. She'd researched his time at school briefly and hadn't found anything of note. Surely she wouldn't have missed something catastrophic.

"It started out well enough," he continued. "We were a rambunctious crew, and needed to cut loose. The ride was just what we needed."

Weston held up a hand to wave the server away as he attempted to return. "Until we decided we didn't want to return to school."

April shifted in her seat, her calf accidentally brushing his as she crossed her legs. The contact caused a rush of heat through her in spite of the boundaries she wanted to keep between them.

"Ever? Or just not that day?"

"Just for the weekend. One of the guys was having a bad week and he convinced us to spend the night out there instead of taking the horses back."

He shook his head. "There was some disagreement, but we'd all thought Zach had been having a rough go, so we figured if it would help him to have a night out with the guys, maybe he'd be the better for it."

"The school must have been worried when you didn't return." She felt the urge to comfort him, since she knew the ending of this story had to be painful. Clearly he hadn't wanted to relive that time in his life if he'd kept the events a secret for so long.

"Probably. But we were sixteen-year-old kids with more testosterone than brains." His fingers rested on the table close to hers.

She couldn't stop herself from laying her palm across the back of his hand. Squeezing lightly.

"By the time the sun was setting," he continued, "we were wound up, pushing each other into risky stunts, telling ourselves we were having the time of our lives. But it rained that night, and I figured everybody would settle down because of that."

"That's not what happened?"

"We slept that night." His mouth twisted in an expression she couldn't read. "But the next morning, some of the guys decided to cliff jump into the local river even though the water level was way too high. We lost the best and brightest among us when our classmate, Zachary Eldridge, jumped into the Arroyo Seco River and never surfaced."

April's heartbeat faltered as she imagined the impact of losing a friend at that age. And in such a traumatic way. She took his hand again and held it. "I'm so sorry."

"We all were." Weston huffed out a long breath, his gaze dropping to their interwoven fingers for a moment before lifting to her face. "We searched for him for hours. Even the search was dangerous." He blinked then and straightened in his seat. "But I only share this story to help you understand Alonzo's role in the aftermath. He was with the search party that found us, and he saw firsthand the kind of condition we were in. He stood by us all through the interrogations by school security and the local police, since the academy didn't want the news to go public."

"Seriously?" How could the school suppress news like that? But they must have, considering she didn't remember seeing any stories about a student death in her research.

"One of the guys' fathers was a political bigwig who did favors for Dowdon. I think they feared repercussions from an important donor more than anything." Still holding her hand, Weston waved to the server with the other.

A waitress quickly emerged from the kitchen with two steaming plates.

April could feel a new anger stirring in her over Weston's story. How could money be more important than a student's life? Than all of their lives, given the profound impact the death must have had on each of the classmates? The boys had deserved professional counseling. They should have had the comfort of their families, not a cover-up to maintain.

"So you feel like Alonzo's actions from that time are indicative of his good character." She tried to see it from Weston's perspective and failed. Anyone involved with that school should have insisted the truth come out.

Although, perhaps there were more factors at work than the father with powerful connections. Public interest in the boy's death might have made the aftermath of the accident even more traumatic for Zach's friends. It was tough enough to grieve something like that privately. How much more difficult would it have been to process in the public eye?

After giving Weston's hand one last squeeze, she withdrew her touch as the waitress laid plates in front of them. The main course was thin-sliced elk medallions drizzled with a blackberry-red wine sauce and garnished with parsley sprigs.

"Alonzo wasn't just an advocate in those weeks after the incident," Weston explained once they were alone again. "He became a trusted friend. A father figure to some of the guys. Me too, I guess, since I never had a good relationship with my dad."

She recalled his strained bond with his brother as well, and found herself wanting to ask more about that. But she wasn't here to follow up on her personal attraction to Weston, no matter how tempting that might be. She had a job to do. And as soon as that was done, she needed to be back home overseeing her mother's health.

With an effort, she forced herself to line up the facts. Alonzo Salazar was allegedly paying for a thirteen-year-old boy's education. Weston didn't think Alonzo had been having an affair with a much younger woman at the time. But perhaps he would support the child of someone he felt close to. If not one of the owners of Mesa Falls Ranch, then who?

"What if the boy Alonzo was supporting turns out to be Zachary's son?"

"No," Weston told her flatly, refilling her wineglass and his own water glass. "Not possible."

"But if Alonzo was close to all six of you, he must have felt a connection to Zach's death. Maybe he wanted to help a son left behind—"

Weston was already shaking his head. "Zach was gay. He'd come out long before that trip. He was comfortable with it—" He stopped himself and looked thoughtful before continuing. "At least, he appeared to be at ease with himself. As comfortable as any guy is with his sexuality at that age."

April didn't know what to think. She'd learned so much today only to have a whole new batch of unanswered questions. And in the meantime, she'd backed Weston into a corner to share a difficult experience from his past. Regret weighed on her even as she sampled the mouthwatering meat. She hadn't meant to pry into something that had to have been so painful.

"Then maybe the father wasn't a student at Dowdon. Nicole Smith's sister could have crossed paths with him some other way." The school was remote, but Alonzo must have made trips into a local town. He probably had friendships beyond the school. She would know more once she had a chance to speak to Nicole at length. "But we still have to assume the father was someone Alonzo might have felt protective of."

"Or else he didn't know the father at all. He simply knew the mother and felt protective of her for whatever reason." Weston stared out over the ice pond outside the barn, his gaze resting on the last couple still skating in the cold. The pair circled each other, laughing.

And then they were kissing.

Slow and lingering.

The moment was an intimate one, and the young man and woman probably didn't even realize anyone else could see them. April averted her eyes, only to realize Weston had switched his focus to her.

Her cheeks heated with sudden awareness. A confusing mix of emotions cascaded through her. Desire for him threaded through it all. Weston had asked her for a kiss the night before—to tease and distract her, she thought. But at the moment, it felt like a missed opportunity.

She would have enjoyed kissing him.

"I'll research more tomorrow." She forced the words past a dry throat, then took a sip of her water to try to cool off. "Thank you for sharing your story with me. I know it can't be easy to relive something like that, but I appreciate the better perspective it gives me on Alonzo."

She needed to reroute her thoughts before she sent Weston any more mixed signals. Gladly, she concentrated on her meal instead of him.

He was silent for a moment as they ate. But then he surprised her by brushing a touch along her shoulder, his palm a warm weight through the thin crepe sleeve of her dress.

"I can't help but wonder if you'll still share evenings like this with me," he said, "if I don't have any more information for your case."

Her pulse sped at his touch. Memories of waking up pressed against him returned with a vengeance.

"I probably shouldn't," she admitted. She was already straddling the line between a personal and professional relationship.

Gray areas in her life made her uncomfortable. And whatever was happening with Weston fell into that blurry place.

"No?" His eyes seemed greener in the firelight as he brushed a curl away from her face and studied her across the small table. "Why not?"

His effect on her was potent. And gaining strength the more time she spent with him.

"It isn't a good practice to get—" she searched for the right words, struggling to ignore the mesmerizing feel of his fingers smoothing the wayward strand

"—to get *close* to someone who figures prominently in a case I'm working."

"I'm well outside the focus of your investigation." He made a relationship between them sound logical when she knew it would be self-indulgent. Impulsive, even.

Still, heat curled in her belly, a teasing warmth. He canted closer, almost near enough to kiss. When did she ever indulge herself?

"It's important that I remain impartial." Had she leaned toward him too? Her words were the softest whisper between them.

"To your work, maybe." His touch skimmed her cheek, tipping her chin up. "But not to me."

For a long, heated moment, she breathed in the tantalizing possibility of pursuing the attraction.

"You're suggesting we keep spending time together." She needed to be very clear about this. No gray areas. What if he was only using their chemistry to keep track of her investigation?

Anxiety spiked along with all that delicious awareness.

"At least let me accompany you to meet my aunt Fallon." His hand lingered along her jaw, making her skin tingle as she contemplated what he was asking. "You wasted a trip to Kalispell at Christmastime when she wasn't home. I can call ahead for us and introduce you."

The woman had been a confidante of Alonzo's in the years before his death. What else might April glean from that interview? She couldn't deny the appeal of more time spent with Weston, even if she risked a certain amount of objectivity.

"You'd make the trip with me?" The drive north had been tense last time, a snowstorm making the ride even longer.

"Yes. I have a home close to her place for when I go see her. We can speak to her, then I'll make you dinner at my place." The potential for more than dinner hung heavy in the air, all the more compelling for how much she wanted to kiss him right now. "Spending the night would, of course, be entirely your call."

"And if I prefer to have my own bedroom?" She realized she was actually considering it. Not just the interview with Fallon Reed, but also a night spent with Weston Rivera.

She felt breathless at the thought.

"Then I would be sure the guest room had fresh sheets. You set the pace, April. But I refuse to pretend that I don't feel something for you." The certainty in his eyes and in his words appealed to her even more than the physical draw of his nearness.

And that spoke volumes. Maybe she could take a chance this once, knowing she'd be leaving Montana soon anyway. She could take this kiss. This chance to feel something more than the endless sense of duty that came with her day-to-day life.

She splayed a palm on his jacket lapel, and leaned closer, ready to claim what she wanted.

"That's a good thing, because I'm not a woman who plays games."

Six

April's kiss disarmed him.

Weston hadn't expected it here, now, during their dinner. But when her lips brushed his, he was only too happy to drink in her sweetness, which held a whole lot more appeal than any five-star meal. Her lips moved in a seductive slide over his, making him forget everything but her. The soft press of her mouth, the taste of red wine and delectable woman, ignited the desire that had been on slow simmer ever since he'd awoken in the tent with his hand cradling her breast. The scorching memory of her body fitted tightly to his took the kiss from zero to sixty in record-setting time.

It was all he could do to ease back, even knowing a waitstaff hovered on the perimeter of the room, their table for two in full view.

"April." He breathed her in after he let her go, wanting more and needing to wait. "I hope that's a yes to a trip to Kalispell."

Belatedly, he remembered her warning—*I'm not a woman who plays games*—and wondered how he could, in good faith, let things go any farther between them if he didn't come clean about all he knew in regard to the past. How could he withhold the truth about his own role in Zach's death?

He'd failed to save his friend. The knowledge chilled him as he pulled away.

"That's a yes." She looked as rattled by the kiss as he felt, her blue gaze darting from his as she took a long drink from her water glass. "I appreciate the ride to Kalispell and the introduction."

He noticed how carefully she reminded him of what she was agreeing to, delineating her expectations. Fine by him. There wasn't a chance he'd let things escalate until he'd figured out how much more of the past he could share with her anyway. Not all of it was his story to tell.

Tonight, he'd have to contact the other owners of Mesa Falls. Warn them that things were snowballing in regard to Alonzo Salazar and the past that tied them all together.

He would have preferred to spend this evening savoring the victory of having gotten closer to April. Instead, the uneasy dance of conflict and desire eclipsed the rest of the meal, reminding him that his first obligation was to the friends who were now his business partners, no matter how much he might wish otherwise.

The kiss was never far from her mind that night.

April twisted restlessly in the Egyptian cotton sheets of her luxury suite in the ranch's main guest lodge, thinking about that devastating moment when Weston Rivera's lips had grazed hers. Setting her on fire.

Thrusting off the covers after failing to fall asleep, she padded across the floor of her room, moonlight shining through the window behind the sofa. She reached to close the curtains, but stopped when she caught a glimpse of the mountains glinting white. Crystalline snowflakes reflecting the white glow made the high peaks look like they'd been dipped in glitter. A magical sight for her even though she lived in Denver. She might be in close proximity to her own stretch of Rockies back home, but her life there seemed confined to her job in the city and her duties for her mother.

Was it any wonder she'd seized on that ill-advised kiss with Weston over dinner? She wouldn't be in Montana much longer. She could at least grab whatever pleasure she could before she returned to her narrow world of obligation. Her long-ago attempt at rebellion as a teen had sent her mother down the path to hoarding in the first place, widening the gulf between her parents that had driven April's father away for good. She wouldn't abandon her mom now, no matter how great the temptation to lose herself in Weston's touch. At least she'd managed to reinstate the cleaning service after a lot of fast talking on the phone to the supervisor in charge. And an increase in their fee.

For now, though, her job here wasn't over yet. Which meant she had a narrow window of time to enjoy herself.

Her phone vibrated with a notification, pulling her attention from the mountains and memories. Hurriedly closing the curtains, she returned to her bed to flip over the device where it was charging on the nightstand. She tucked her cold toes under the covers again as she read a message from Nicole Smith. April had texted her shortly before bed, asking her to share any physical evidence of her claims and requesting a time to speak again at length.

Can't meet tomorrow. My supervisor subbed me last minute as ranch support staff on a three-day cattle expo in LA. Will text when I return. If I can find any of my sister's bank statements with past deposits from the trust for Matthew, I will forward them.

Frustration balled in April's gut. Three days? She briefly contemplated contacting her boss or the client to request travel fees to confront Nicole in Los Angeles. But until she had proof of support money being paid by Alonzo, that wasn't fair to her client. April knew better than to chase phantom leads. No, her best bet was to accept Weston's invitation to meet with his aunt—a woman who'd been close to Alonzo.

A visit to Kalispell would be the right move for her case. The fact that she would be spending more time with Weston Rivera—possibly overnight in his mountain home—didn't weigh into her decision at all.

Yet she couldn't deny that the thought of it made her heart beat faster.

Seated beside April in his Land Rover the next day, Weston headed north on 35 along Flathead Lake toward Kalispell. He'd called his aunt the night before, and Fallon had encouraged him to come for a visit soon, since she planned an extended trip to Costa Rica at the end of the month.

So when April had messaged him this morning, her schedule cleared for the rest of the week, he'd been only too glad to make the journey today. Weston had gotten in touch with his property manager to prepare the house for them in case they stayed in Kalispell overnight, but he suspected April would want to return to Mesa Falls once he shared more of the details about Zach's death. She'd been incensed over dinner last night when she'd heard how the story had been kept out of the news. What would she think once she learned of the role he himself had played?

Fourteen years hadn't been enough time to forgive himself. He sure didn't expect April to feel the same way about him with only hours to process what he was about to tell her. But he'd cleared the path to discuss the details, at least, after sending an email to the other ranch owners the night before. He'd given them all fair warning that interest in Alonzo was heating up and that Devon Salazar's investigative firm wouldn't quit until they had answers. He hadn't shared anything about the mystery child connected to Alonzo, though. With no concrete evidence of the boy's paternity yet, Weston wouldn't stir the pot unnecessarily.

The only response he'd received to his email had been from fellow owner Gage Striker, who'd told Weston to share whatever he deemed reasonable. That was it. A one-sentence reply that had given Weston the green light to topple the barriers they'd all kept around that summer for the whole of their adult lives. While Weston appreciated Gage's confidence in his judgment about what to share, he also hated being the only one on-site in Montana if the media decided the old story was worth revisiting.

Now, with time dwindling before they reached Kalispell, he knew he should talk to April. Glancing over at her across the Land Rover's wide console, he took in her black pantsuit with tiny gold buttons to the waist. She'd removed her wool coat an hour into the trip, folding and stowing it in the back seat with his. The heated leather seats kept the interior warm despite the frigid temperature outside.

She tipped up her sunglasses and met his gaze, perching the shades on her head, blond curls spilling over her shoulders.

"Thank you for making the trip today." She drew some staticky hair away from her shoulder, a few strands clinging to the window next to her, leaping with a life of their own. "I felt like our evening together took an awkward turn after I kissed you, and I thought maybe you'd back out."

In spite of the dark cloud of his thoughts hanging over him, he had to admire her forthrightness. Some women might have danced around a realization like that.

"It's not awkward." He shook his head, regretting that she'd read his mixed feelings even as he appreciated her willingness to confront the topic. "At least, not because of the kiss."

His grip tightened on the heated steering wheel; he recognized that she'd given him an opening for that conversation he didn't want to have.

"So you admit there was some awkwardness?" She sounded more curious than anything, and for that he was grateful.

"Only because I realized that I wanted more than just a kiss." He followed the shore road around a winding turn, slowing for a few deer crossing a quiet stretch.

Three does stared at the Land Rover before leaping back into the woods on the east side of the highway. April drummed her short fingernails softly on the gray leather console. Once. Twice.

"I don't see why that's a problem." She shook her head as if his behavior was another complex problem to solve. "If you are worried that I'm going to have any expectations of you after my case closes, Weston, you couldn't be more wrong."

"I wasn't thinking about that." He pressed the accelerator, frustration with himself firing faster than the engine. This beautiful, intelligent woman seemed to be openly welcoming a no-strings affair, and instead of embracing it like he wanted to, he had to clear the air. Talk about things he'd hoped never to revisit. "But I realized it wasn't fair to you to move forward with the attraction when I wasn't completely honest yesterday. I brushed over details of Zach's story that are important."

Tugging the sunglasses off her head, she folded them precisely and set them in a depression in the console, an action that seemed to buy her time before she responded.

"In my work, I'm frequently faced with puzzles that unravel slowly at first and then—all at once." She swung her gaze toward him. "So I can't say I'm surprised to have the story come together in pieces."

He ground his teeth together, hating the image of himself as cagey. "The facts weren't all mine to share. I wanted to touch base with some of the people who might be affected by the outcome of this if the past comes to light."

"Fair enough." She accepted his explanation with a nod while he drove around the bend in a village so small it was just a few buildings nestled in the snow. "What else should I know?"

He slowed down for an older man bundled in bulky layers crossing the street. The guy clamped his fedora hat to his head with a leather-gloved hand as he battled the gusts coming off the frozen lake.

Weston knew there was no way around the topic now. He'd have to put his head into the wind as surely as the old guy did and forge his way through.

"The reason we all agreed with the school's decision not to share Zach's death with the press," he began, coming right to the point. "The reason we didn't want that kind of spotlight was because we weren't sure if his cliff dive was truly an accident or if—" Even all these years later, the idea was raw as a fresh wound. "He might have jumped that day—when the water was too high after a storm—because he wanted to end his life."

Weston's blood rushed in his ears, just like the water had when he'd jumped in after Zach to try to save him. For a moment, he couldn't hear anything but his own breathing. Not a surprise, given that he hadn't shared the story with anyone since the psychologist the school had demanded he see right after the incident. The therapist hadn't been able to excise his nightmares, but at least he'd gained some techniques for pulling his thoughts from the dark rat maze of guilt.

"I'm so sorry, Weston." April's gentle words floated through his consciousness before he grew aware of her touch on his shoulder, the gentle squeeze of her fingers. "I can understand how that ambiguity would have complicated the family's decision to release more information."

"Zach had a poor excuse for family," Weston found himself saying, steering through another winding section of the shore road. "He attended Dowdon on a scholarship because he was bright and talented. His only support system was us—his friends. And we failed him in the end."

He picked up speed as they left behind another village, the vehicle easily navigating the fresh snow blowing off the lake, white puffs swirling past like winter tumbleweeds. April's comforting touch fell away as the vehicle listed to the right on a hard turn.

"You didn't fail him." April's words were firm. Certain. "You all supported him when he wanted to extend the trip in the first place. You tried to be good friends."

Her take on it was flawed because it was based on the barest of details. And yet her perspective was interesting just because it wasn't weighed down by personal involvement.

She hadn't leaped into icy-cold water to find a friend whose body was long gone.

"We didn't see it that way." He'd never shed the guilt that came from his inability to save his friend. "I jumped in after Zach, but I couldn't find him. I couldn't stand knowing that I might have saved him if I knew more about rescue. I took classes in CPR. Courses in water rescue and survival. Even after I finished college, I spent more time in training exercises than I did working my father's ranch." Much to his family's frustration.

"You jumped too?" April asked slowly. "I thought you said the water was too high from a recent storm?"

The rushing waters had been over two feet deeper than they'd been the day before. Murky with debris and mud from the river floor.

"Someone had to pull him out." From the time they were kids, Weston had been the freewheeling daredevil. The prodigal son. The brother who was more expendable. "In our group, I was the risk taker. So when all eyes turned to me, I didn't think twice."

"How terrifying." April's voice was a whisper. "I can't begin to imagine what you went through." She turned and looked out the window as they passed a sign for Kalispell.

"The harder part was getting back out of the water." He'd been numb with cold, his skin shredded with cuts from the branches and rocks swept into the fast current. Still, he wouldn't have left the water without finding Zach if he hadn't floated up on a rock ledge where he'd been too exhausted to fight his friends as they dragged him out. "Because that meant admitting my failure. I had to concede our friend was gone forever, and that I'd been a poor choice to save him."

* * *

April heard the pain in his voice.

She heard it, not because anything gave it away in his tone. Anyone else listening to his account might think him dispassionate. Aloof, even, given how sparing he was with the details. But she recognized the deep ache behind the words because she'd felt it so often herself over the role she'd played in her mother's decline. How easy it was to pinpoint others' misplaced guilt, and yet how impossible to admit the very same guilt was unwarranted when it came to yourself.

"If any of your other friends had gone in the water to look for him, would you have blamed them for returning without Zach?" she ventured, needing to offer him whatever comfort she could.

"Of course not." His answer was immediate. Clear. "And some of them did end up in the water before we had to give up the search, but they climbed down the rocks to enter from water level."

While Weston had been swimming all that time on his own. It chilled her to think what that must have been like. The fear for himself as well as his friend.

Weston downshifted as they reached the outskirts of Kalispell and headed west. When his hand returned to the console between them, April slid her palm over his.

"It wasn't their fault they didn't find him because they were kids. Just like you were," she offered gently as the vehicle began to ascend higher into the mountains.

He opened his mouth to argue—or at least, she guessed that's what he was about to do—so she continued.

"I only mention it because I'm well versed in how easy it can be to blame yourself for things when you're smart, competent and used to bending the world to your will. I carry a lot of guilt over my mother's sickness. And it doesn't matter how many people—doctors, even—have said it's not my fault. I know I bear blame."

Frowning, he took an icy curve very slowly as the road got rougher.

"That's different." His words were clipped. Abrupt.

She brushed a last light touch over his hand before easing back.

"It is, but only because I have the benefit of other people in my hometown knowing the full story, and they weigh in on it. Whereas you haven't had anyone to tell you it's misguided of you to heap all that responsibility on yourself." She glanced over at his clenched jaw, knowing she risked pushing him away by telling him a hard truth, but she felt like he deserved to hear it. "As someone looking at your situation with fresh eyes, I see it so differently than you do. Your friend's death wasn't your fault."

For a long moment, silence reigned, interrupted

only by the hum of the heater and the crackle of ice under the tires.

When he pulled off the road and onto a private drive where the snow was deeper, she saw a huge log cabin home in the distance.

His or his aunt's?

But she didn't have time to ask before he put the SUV in Park and turned to face her. Having his full attention was a sudden intimacy she hadn't been ready for, and his hazel eyes seemed to see inside her.

"Your mother's disorder is a mental illness, April." His tone was kind, even if his words implied their situations weren't the least bit similar. "How could you think you played a role in that?"

"Life stress can be a trigger." She'd caused the stressful situation that started it all. "So what begins as a pattern of comfort—collecting things for enjoyment—spirals into an out-of-control need to acquire."

"And you think you caused that life stress?" he asked, his voice a warm baritone. He raised a disbelieving eyebrow.

"I know I did." Her voice came out tighter, more clipped than she'd intended. But she didn't want to share this story.

"I already bared my soul on this road trip." His smile was wry but humorless. "Am I going to be the only one?"

He had a point.

Gritting her teeth, she tried to frame her words

so this would be as brief as possible. Most of all, she didn't want to sound self-pitying over something that had happened a lifetime ago. "My parents were having problems when I was a teen. My father all but disappeared from our lives, and I resented him for that."

Weston stopped her short with a squeeze to the hand. "Of course you did. You deserve to have your dad in your life."

"I understand that now. But then? I acted out for attention in a way was both predictable and childish. I scandalized my high school—where Mom worked as a teacher—by getting caught in a compromising position with an older student during an event she was chaperoning." Putting it that way was a kindness to herself that April didn't deserve. She'd lured the teen there, knowing full well they'd get caught. She hadn't been thinking about him and his reputation, only considering her own ends. "I coaxed him into the coat closet at the dance and let things get out of hand. I thought my mom would find us and have a reason to call my dad. It would be a way to bond with him in their worry about me." She'd been thoughtless. Stupid. "Instead, the principal found us."

Her ears burned even though she'd long ago grappled with how she'd embarrassed herself and her family by engaging in behavior that would hurt her mother's career. She'd gone to family counseling with her mother, and it had helped April tremendously even if it never seemed to work for her mother.

"That sounds as painful for you as it must have been for her," Weston pointed out, kindness in his voice. "Besides, the stress of your mom's situation existed before that."

April's therapist had made a similar observation. Not that it relieved her of the responsibility for her own actions.

"Yes." She nodded, willing her embarrassment to subside since she knew Weston wasn't judging her. "I just made it a hundred times worse by making her work world miserable. My actions robbed my mother of her most reliable support system— her teacher friends and the school community. The gossip was bad enough. The administrative inquiry into my mother's suitability to chaperone students made her workplace unbearable to the point where she turned in her resignation."

Things had fallen apart after that. Completely and utterly. The anxiety had pushed her mother to the breaking point.

"She made the decision to quit." Weston threaded his fingers through hers, his palm warming her when she hadn't realized a chill had taken hold. "So I'll remind you of what you told me. You were a kid too. It wasn't all on you."

"Intellectually, I know that. But I lo.st a lot of time to negative thoughts over the years, my brain playing the great game of what-if." She stared down at their locked fingers, a new warmth stealing into her despite the conversation she didn't want to be having.

She appreciated the quiet acceptance. The comfort of his presence.

"I've gone a few rounds of that in my day." His slow nod was full of understanding.

"Mom could have recovered from a divorce, if that had been all she'd faced. Without a reason to get up for work every day, she turned to home shopping, filling up our house with things that never had a chance of making her happy." April didn't want this conversation to turn any darker than it already had. Especially now that it appeared they'd arrived at their destination. "But I've made some peace with my guilt—misplaced or not—by taking an active role in helping Mom get better."

"Thank you for sharing that with me." He lifted her hand to his lips and kissed the backs of her fingers. "I know it wasn't easy. Guilt is a relentless beast, and it doesn't play fair."

The pleasure of his mouth against her skin soothed the confusing emotions churning through her, narrowing her focus to that place where they touched. Where his lips lingered.

Her pulse sped, and she remembered what it had been like to kiss him the night before. That moment when their mouths met had been seared into her brain so vividly she'd relived it over and over in her dreams.

"I'm very ready to think about other things," she

confessed, her voice breathless enough to betray what he did to her. She swallowed hard and tried to recover her composure for the interview she needed to conduct with Fallon Reed. "Is that your aunt's house up ahead?"

They were parked in the snowy driveway, the big log cabin–style home visible through a thin layer of fresh powder on the windshield.

"No. I thought you might want to drop our things off and stretch your legs before we meet my aunt." His hazel eyes locked with hers while heat steamed over her skin. "This place belongs to me."

Seven

After the intense conversation on the ride to Kalispell, Weston had figured it would do them both good to retreat to separate corners for an hour or two before they went to visit his aunt.

But he hadn't counted on the sensual turn things would take as they sat in the snow-covered Land Rover, sharing confidences. By the time he unlocked the front door and invited April inside the mountain cabin, the undercurrent of desire between them was palpable.

"This is beautiful," she murmured, taking in the rustic details and minimalist furnishings as he led her to the guest suite at the back of the log home. "The views are breathtaking."

She paused by a window overlooking the Flathead Valley and Swan mountain range. He set her suitcase inside the guest suite, holding the door for her.

"You've got a good view from your bedroom too." His gaze scoured the place, making sure his caretaker had readied everything. Fresh towels waited on the en suite bathroom vanity, and there was a vase of yellow tulips on the nightstand. A basket of toiletries and teas was on the wet bar. "You should have everything you need."

Tearing her gaze from the mountains, she joined him in the guest suite, setting her handbag on the leather love seat before spinning in a circle to take it all in.

Weston couldn't see anything but her, though. Her black pantsuit and boots were sleekly elegant, her blond curls hugging her shoulders as she turned. But he wouldn't let himself act on attraction yet, even though the need to taste her again was a constant thirst.

At one point during their drive, she'd suggested she might be open to a no-strings affair, implying that he didn't need to worry about any expectations from her once she closed her case in Montana. But that had been before he'd shared the full story of his role in Zach's death. They'd both bared more of themselves than they'd wanted to, and that complicated things. Walking away wouldn't be easy if their emotions got tangled up in this.

"If this was my house, I'd never leave it." She ran

a hand along the whitewashed log wall, then bent to sniff the tulips, a smile curving her lips when she straightened. "Do you come up here often?"

"Not as much the last two years, since I started overseeing Mesa Falls." He should leave her now that he'd shown her the suite, but his boots seemed nailed to the floor.

He could still feel the softness of her skin against his lips from when he'd kissed the back of her hand. Still smell the hint of flowers and spices that scented her skin.

Maybe his thoughts showed in his expression, because the silence stretched out between them, awareness crowding the suite. April folded her arms, opening her mouth to speak and then closing it.

The second time she tried, she blurted, "I should get ready."

"Of course. I should, as well." He nodded, giving her space even though that was the last thing he wanted. He wanted her in his arms, his lips fastened to hers as he kissed his fill. "And we can drive back to the ranch tonight if you like. It's your call."

"I know. And thank you for that." Her tone softened, the stiffness in her shoulders easing a fraction. Her mouth twisted in a wry smile. "I'm more concerned that if I don't get ready for a visit to your aunt's place now, we won't make it out of the house tonight at all."

Her words, so unexpected and so wholly welcome, shot a jolt of pure lust through him. The idea that she was thinking along the same lines as him, that the attraction was every bit as unwieldy for her, threatened to torch the last of his restraint. And yet, the notion served as a reminder that business came first with April. She wouldn't sacrifice her work for personal pleasure. Logically, he applauded that. It kept them on the same page. Ensured they understood one another.

But no matter how often life had taught him to be disciplined and focused, a part of him wondered what it might be like to not overthink what was happening between them. To follow the heat and attraction and to hell with the consequences.

"Just let me know when you're ready," he managed as he finally unfastened his feet from the floor. "And I'll gladly show you how good things could be between us."

Turning on his boot heel, he walked out and closed the door behind him.

An hour later, April tried to put the simmering attraction to Weston out of her mind as she accepted a cup of tea in a mug covered with butterflies from his aunt Fallon. Seated beside him in the living room of Fallon Reed's Alpine-style chalet perched high over the town of Kalispell, it wasn't easy to forget that she planned to spend the night with him.

He seemed to take up all the space in Fallon's small living area, his long legs and broad shoulders within touching distance as he and April shared a love seat. They'd had no choice but to sit there, since the only other chair in the room was Fallon's recliner with her sweater draped over the back and her cross-word puzzle in progress on the seat. With steel-gray hair in a pixie cut and big sunflower earrings, their hostess seemed an interesting study in contrasts. Her leggings and long cashmere sweater were fashionably cut and modern, the fabric expensive-looking. High-end dishes sat on the open shelving beside a collection of campy salt and pepper shakers shaped like woodland creatures. Postcards from far-flung destinations decorated a corkboard near the front entrance.

"Thank you," April told her as she held the butterfly mug, her fingers savoring the warmth.

A fire burned low in the painted brick hearth, but April still hadn't warmed up from their trek through the snow to the front door.

"Are you sure you won't stay for supper?" Fallon asked as she poured a cup for herself. "I don't have much here, but we can head into town—"

"We've made plans already, but thank you." Weston rose from the love seat to stir the fire, adding another log from the basket sitting next to it. The flames rose, sending a gratifying wave of heat into the room. "It was kind enough of you to see us on such short notice."

Fallon waved away the words as she returned to the living room in her stocking feet, carrying her mug over to the recliner. "You never need an invitation, Weston. It's always a pleasure to spend time with you."

"I'm going to grab some more firewood for you." Straightening from the hearth, he stalked toward a back door April hadn't noticed before. "April can tell you about her case."

After sipping her tea, April hastily set aside the mug, placing it on the wooden tray resting on a trunk that served as a coffee table. She hadn't expected to be thrust into the spotlight right away.

"Of course." She tore her gaze from Weston as he went outdoors without his coat, and turned her full attention to his aunt. "I'm not sure how much Weston told you—"

"He said your firm has been hired to track Alonzo Salazar's finances." Fallon launched right into the topic as she crossed her legs, her manicured fingers wrapping around her mug. One pink nail tapped a ceramic butterfly thoughtfully. "I'm not sure how much I can help you, since Alonzo and I were good friends but not the kind of friends who asked those sorts of questions of one another."

"I'm also trying to track where he traveled." April had learned long ago to ask more indirect questions in interviews like this. People often thought they knew nothing when they had helpful pieces of the puzzle without knowing it. "Do you know where he spent time when he wasn't with you or in his West Coast home?"

Hopefully, she could find leads in those cities.

"That I can help you with." Fallon pointed toward the front door. "At least half of my postcards are from trips Alonzo and I took together. He was the one who started me on the path to the humanitarian work I do now."

Surprised, April's focus moved to the corkboard. "May I take a look?"

"Please do," Fallon offered, rising from her chair and hurrying toward the back door, where Weston was shouldering his way inside, snow-covered and arms full of split logs.

April watched their easy interaction, Fallon chiding him for doing the job and Weston insisting he wasn't done yet. There was obviously a warm family connection between them, the comfort of people who'd spent a lot of time together. It surprised her a bit, since his relationship with his immediate family sounded so strained. Tearing her gaze from Weston's broad shoulders as he moved through the living room, April focused on the postcards as she neared the narrow hall table under the display board.

Photos from rural Mexico and Argentina were pinned beside pictures of cities in South Africa and Poland. April turned a few over and saw they all were dated. A card from the Philippines read, "Torres house, January 2015," and underneath that, someone had scrawled an address in Luzon. The back of another postcard from Egypt read, "Antoun house, August 2016," with an address in a place called Al Minia.

While Weston stacked firewood, April took photos of the board and several postcards.

"Finding everything you need, hon?" Fallon called from the fireplace, where she was moving her poker set to make room for more logs.

"You mentioned humanitarian projects." April spotted a photo of Fallon—before she had gray hair—with an arm draped around Alonzo Salazar. They were dressed in overalls and T-shirts, smiling in front of a small house and flanked by a young man and his very pregnant wife. "Like what?"

"Alonzo gave a lot of time to building homes for people in need." Fallon joined April by the corkboard as Weston went back outdoors for another load of kindling. "Sometimes he worked on bigger projects like developing clean water systems for small villages, but he was so good at building houses and getting the beneficiary families involved that he ended up working on those the most."

April's vision of Alonzo shifted yet again. Had he given his time, or money too? The financial records she'd seen hadn't hinted at donations to these kinds of causes, but perhaps he'd funneled some of the book revenue in that direction. If he was genuinely sorry for writing *Hollywood Newlyweds* and causing the family it was based on so much grief, perhaps contributing to a charitable effort eased the guilt.

"How did the two of you meet?" April asked, not just out of social politeness, but because it could give her a better picture of their relationship.

Anxiety flitted through her that she didn't normally feel at this point in her cases. These people were so real to her now, and Weston was becoming important in a way she hadn't counted on.

"When Weston started spending more time in Mesa Falls, I went down there to check out the place for myself. Alonzo was staying there that week too, and we ended up bonding over an interest in travel." Fallon smiled as she traced the photo of the two of them together with her finger. "He'd already done so many of the things I was interested in doing—making a difference in the world. Giving back. When he suggested I go with him on his next trip to build houses in Mexico, I laughed at first. But he was completely serious."

"And you went?" April turned to study her hostess more carefully, searching the woman's face for any resemblance to Weston, but finding none.

"Not that trip. But he sent me postcards, and we started emailing more. By the end of that year, I joined a larger trip to the Philippines and got hooked on good works." Fallon glanced over her shoulder toward the back door, where Weston has disappeared outside. "I'm not sure how much you know about Weston's family, but the Riveras aren't the most giving people. Weston and I get along because we aren't like them. But his mother—my sister—has always been driven to let the world know she's wealthy and successful, and she married a man who is the same way. Weston is a black sheep in that clan, but believe me, that's a good thing."

The back door opened again, and a blast of cold air accompanied Weston into the chalet. He was hardworking. Steady. Quietly taking care of his aunt without being asked. All of those things appealed to April so much.

He took one look at them together and shook his head.

"You're not filling her ears with stories about my family." He used his foot to shut the door behind him, then toed off his snowy boots on the mat.

"I just outlined the basics." Fallon didn't sound at all apologetic, but she did hurry over to help him, taking a couple of logs from the top of the armful he carried. "I thought she should be forewarned."

Weston shook his head while he stacked the new batch of wood. "I live three states away from them so I don't have to worry about it, remember?"

The two of them bickered in a friendly way that April envied. And she felt the draw of him so strongly she had to look over more postcards to distract herself. She snapped a few last pictures. She could find travel records now that she had dates and knew where to look. The visit had been beneficial to her case even if it had added another confusing layer to her relationship with Weston.

What had caused the divide in his family? And did it extend to the brother who remained a part owner of Mesa Falls Ranch and, she supposed,

Weston's friend? She wasn't sure how to ask, especially when they'd already shared painful pieces of their pasts today. She guessed he wasn't any more eager to wade into those waters again than she was.

When they left Fallon's house, his hand on her elbow, the temptation to be with him ramped up all over again. The desire to lean in, to be close. Once they were alone again, she knew he would confront her about what she wanted to do next. They could have dinner and then drive back to Mesa Falls. Or they could have dinner and spend the night.

He'd made it clear the decision was hers. That even if she wanted to spend the night in Kalispell, she had her own room and her own space.

But did she want to be alone?

Watching Weston take care of his aunt, April felt a new longing for him, something far outside the ever-present physical attraction. He was a giving man—something that Fallon had spelled out in no uncertain terms. He had a conscience about being unable to save his friend, and he'd gone into volunteer rescue work to save others.

And beyond all that, he'd rescued April on a mountaintop when he didn't have to. When he'd been trying to stay away from her.

She saw that act in a new light now, understanding him better. For a woman who was used to bearing her family burdens, the one who did the giving, it was a heady new feeling to have someone sacrifice for her.

She didn't want to be alone tonight. Not when she had the chance to know Weston Rivera's touch.

If only just this once.

On the road from Fallon's house back to his retreat cabin, Weston glanced over at his lovely but silent passenger. Squinting in the low light from the setting sun, he acknowledged that April wasn't an easy woman to read. Had her investigative work taught her the impassive observation skills she employed so easily? He hated to think that her life experience—the teenage stunt that had gone so awry for her—had resulted in her becoming more of a bystander to her life than an active participant.

But there was no denying that she seemed reserved tonight. Introspective.

"You've been quiet since we left Fallon's," Weston noted after he'd pulled into the long driveway that led to his cabin. "Are you having second thoughts about staying in Kalispell? We can get back on the road if you prefer."

He'd been thinking about kissing her again all day long, his hunger becoming even more insistent after he'd shared the details from his past and she hadn't seemed to judge him harshly for his failures. Her acceptance had made him rethink what he wanted out of their time together, and he couldn't deny that—more than anything—he wanted her.

"No second thoughts here," she assured him as he parked the Land Rover in the double garage. "I was just thinking through my next steps on the investigation so I can set work aside for the night."

Her words sparked along his skin, igniting a flame he hadn't wanted to fan until he was certain how she wanted the night to end.

"That sounds promising." He shut off the engine and moved to the passenger side of the vehicle to open her door, stepping around the snowy tracks left by the tire treads.

She took his hand and let him help her down, her boots stepping close to his. The overhead light in the garage cast uneven shadows, but he caught a flash of something like anticipation in her blue gaze.

"How about we ban all work conversation over dinner?" she suggested, not moving away from him. "No talking about Salazars or finances."

"Excellent idea." He shifted his hold on her hand, threading his fingers deliberately through hers. Squeezing. "While we're at it, we could rule out discussion of our pasts too. Live in the moment."

A smile hitched at the corner of her lips.

"This is sounding better all the while. Although I'm not entirely sure I know how to live in the moment if I'm not climbing a mountain."

It clicked in his head then why she loved climbing. Why she'd seemed different on the mountain—less reserved. Freer, somehow. She left her cares behind when she hiked, forgetting about all the things that tethered her to her day-to-day life.

He could understand that. He'd logged plenty of miles running from his own demons.

"I know how to fix that," he assured her, drawing her with him toward the entrance to the house. "I've got a surefire way to keep you anchored in the present."

She followed him up two steps and through the door to the mudroom. Inside, a motion light clicked on to illuminate the muted gray travertine tiles and wrought iron coat hooks on the walls, a slim mirror reflecting the image of the two of them.

"You do?" She let go of his hand to shrug off her coat, but he took over the task for her, forcing his hands not to linger on her shoulders. He hung the long wool trench on a hook beside his shearling jacket. "I've tried meditation, but I'm not good at it."

He laughed lightly, returning to her side even though he knew he should start dinner. They'd had a long day, and he wanted to be a good host.

But he'd been ignoring the need for her for hours, and every moment he spent with her wound him tighter.

"Meditation isn't going to do the job." He shook his head and stepped closer to her, contemplating the vision she made in her elegant black pantsuit and the long, wild curls that had rebelled more as the day wore on. Her hair had grown springier and fuller.

"No?" Her eyes tracked him, darting back and forth, as if she couldn't quite figure out what was next.

"No." He couldn't wait to touch her any longer,

so he didn't. He slid his hands under all that luscious hair, letting it tickle his knuckles while his fingers splayed over her shoulders and back. Breathing deep, he caught a hint of her fragrance, something subtly spicy and vaguely floral too. "If you want to feel the present moment, to really dwell in the here and now, you need to make the moment memorable. Make it worth cataloging every minute detail."

Sliding one of his feet between hers, he let himself feel the heat of her body close to his without pressing himself against her. He felt a warm, delectable anticipation of what was to come.

Her eyes widened, her lips rounding into a small, silent *O* of either acknowledgment or surprise. Her breath huffed over his mouth, scented with mint and lemongrass tea. Her lips were bare, the natural pink color calling for closer examination before he could describe it.

He looked forward to that. But first, he lowered his voice for close range, stroking a finger just beneath the curve of her jaw.

"The secret to making a moment last, April," he confided, his whole body tense with wanting. Waiting. "Is kissing."

Eight

April couldn't have said who moved first.

It was like laying a match to dry tinder, and they both caught flame at the same moment. In an instant, their mouths met. Fused.

This kiss was nothing like the one she'd given him over dinner, when she'd seized her courage and tasted a few moments of pleasure. This time, he licked into her mouth, igniting a raw passion that stole her breath. It was everything she wanted. Everything she needed for this night.

She slid her hands up his arms, steadying herself on his shoulders as she swayed into him. His powerful body anchored her when the pleasure of the kiss threatened to pull her under. Consume her. She held on to him, knowing he wouldn't let go even though he seemed as lost in this moment as she was.

She felt his hands stroking through her hair, down her spine, splaying over the arch of her back. All of those touches brought her closer, sealing her body to his, making her ache for still more of him. Just one kiss, and she was melting inside her clothes, desperate to be free of them.

So when he eased back, she didn't even comprehend what was happening. Her grip tightened on his shoulders for a moment, fingers clenching the fabric of his white button-down.

"I don't want to rush things—"

"You're not." She realized that she hadn't even let him get a full sentence out. Biting her lip, she forced her fingers to relax their grip, to ease away an inch. "That is, I don't feel rushed."

He arched an eyebrow, his hazel gaze sweeping over her before he lowered his voice. "Is this happening then?"

The growl in his tone made her toes curl inside her boots. She could have purred with pleasure at the thought of being with him.

"From my point of view," she said, wanting to spell it out as clearly as she knew how, needing to make sure they understood each other, "it can't happen soon enough."

"That sounds like a challenge." He contemplated her for the space of a heavy heartbeat. And then another.

Was he waiting for her to contradict him? She had no intention of doing any such thing.

Then, before she knew what he was about, his hands slid around her hips, lifting her against him. He spun her in his arms, backing her against the door they'd just entered. A barrier had tumbled between them, and not just a physical one. She had a glimpse of the more reckless heart beneath his tightly controlled actions, and it thrilled her as much as the heated press of his body.

His tongue plunged into her mouth, and she wrapped her legs around his hips. At the press of his erection, she wriggled closer still. His hand cradled her face, steadying her for his kiss, angling her chin where he wanted her.

And oh, his mouth. The things he did with it elicited sensations everywhere. A shiver tripped up her spine.

She squeezed her thighs tighter, locking her heels with a moan that made his hips buck against her. Sweet tension coiled inside her, along with the need to undress him. She broke the kiss long enough to inform him, "We need less clothes."

"We are of one mind tonight," he assured her, straightening enough to lift her again.

She clung to him, arms around his neck, only half-focused on where they were going. His bedroom, she guessed, since he headed in a different direction than the suite he'd shown her earlier. They went through a hallway where recessed lighting cast shadows on his face that accented his high cheekbones and sharp jaw. She bent to kiss him there, feeling the slight bristle of his cheek, inhaling the fading scent of teakwood aftershave as he stepped into the wide expanse of his bedroom, where the whitewashed log walls framed a massive espresso-colored bed draped in pale gray linens. The only illumination in the room came from a spotlight on a canvas painting of a wooded mountainside covered in snow.

He kicked the door shut behind them, and she edged back to see his expression, but he was completely focused on the bed.

Anticipation curled through her as he lowered them both onto it. His knees hit the mattress along with her hips. Her fingers flew to the buttons on his shirt, working fast. She was desperate to feel his skin against hers. Hell, desperate just to see him.

He felt so incredibly good beneath his clothes. She unfastened and tugged, dragging the shirt down his shoulders as she gave thanks to the light in the room for giving her a glimpse of so much masculine strength. Lean muscles worked in smooth harmony as he moved over her, unfastening the hooks on her jumpsuit.

Every now and then, a knuckle grazed her skin. Between her breasts first. Then on her upper stomach. Her navel. He paused there, as if deliberating. But when he yanked his gaze up to meet hers, she realized he was only thinking about how to proceed. Anticipating her as much as she was longing for him.

She drew in a breath, holding on to the moment. And in that instant, he stepped away from her, freeing himself from her legs. Yet as soon as she missed the feel of him there, he was on his knees next to the bed, his shoulders making room between her thighs even as his hand raked down the top half of her outfit.

Oh.

She'd never survive his undressing as he kissed his way down the fastenings. He hovered at the jumpsuit hook above her panties, his breath warm enough for her to feel it through the layers of lace and silk. Pleasure spiked along with her heart rate. Her fingers twisted in the gray cotton of the duvet, holding tight.

And then his lips were there, molding to her skin before his tongue teased along the waistband of her underwear. Slid beneath.

Her breath came faster, all of her focus narrowed to the places his tongue touched. By the time he dragged her panties down and off along with the rest of her clothes, her skin tingled everywhere, nerve endings buzzing. The tender scrape of his jaw against her inner thigh made her heartbeat stutter. When he kissed her intimately, tasting and exploring with a thoroughness that shattered all reserve, her release pulsed through her in wave after wave of pleasure.

He hugged her hips, holding her there, coaxing every last twitch of delicious fulfillment from her body. Afterward, wrung out and sated, she blinked up at him as he straightened. Dimly aware he hadn't even finished undressing, she dragged a pillow closer while she watched him retrieve a condom and shed his clothes.

Seeing his heavy male muscles shifting under his skin stirred a hunger in her all over again. The dim light cast shadows that highlighted the ridges of his abs, the delineation in his arms. As soon as he came within touching distance, she skimmed her finger-tip down one of his shoulders to skate over the taut triceps while he stretched out above her on the bed.

Hazel eyes locked on hers, he made room for him-self between her legs. The heat and weight of his erection brushed over her thigh just long enough to remind her how much more she still wanted from him. She arched up to kiss him, urging him closer until he nudged his way inside her. Slowly.

Incredibly.

He remained still for a long moment, letting her adjust. She slid her arms around him, holding on to the moment when it felt like there was nothing else in the world but this. Them.

Once he started to move, she blinked her eyes open, realizing how quickly she could lose herself in everything she felt inside. She flexed her fingers tighter into his shoulders, needing to remain focused on the physical. The outward. The pleasure.

They moved together, legs tangling, arms twin-ing, grappling for purchase as they rolled from one side to the other. She kissed him, fingers combing through his hair and then spearing up the back of his neck to rake the silky strands all over again.

When he shifted her on top of him, she bent forward to trail kisses along his chest, teasing and tasting her way around the muscles there. Seized with the need to make him feel all of the bliss that he'd given her, she captured his hands and pinned them lightly above his head. She admired the splay of his shoulders, took in the arched, curious eyebrow as he no doubt wondered what she was doing. Then she set about finding what he liked best.

Slow undulations of her hips drove them both higher. She sensed her own release was close again, but before she could drive them both there, he flipped her to her back. Their eyes met, and the look in his made her breath catch.

He hovered above her for a long moment, and when their bodies joined fully again, an orgasm shook her to her toes. He followed her a moment later, the sensations spiraling on and on between them until they lay in a heap of spent limbs and damp skin in the cooling air.

A languid peacefulness stole over her as her heart stopped racing and settled into a normal rhythm again. Their breathing synced up, and she nuzzled deeper into the pillow, replete. Weston moved to drag a blanket over her, kissing her shoulder as he swiped stray curls from her cheek.

"I'm going to make you dinner," he told her softly. "I feel like a bad host for not feeding you earlier."

"On the contrary, you've been an extremely attentive host." A smile hitched at her lips even though she felt a twinge of worry that he was easing away from her so soon. "I won't complain about how you've spent your time tonight."

She should be relieved that he was giving her some space to process what had just happened between them. But the regret she felt at not being able to curl against him told her she was letting her emotions get too tangled up in him already. Tugging the blanket under her chin, she rolled on her back to see him better as he dragged on a pair of jeans.

Commando.

"Nevertheless," he told her as he pulled a clean T-shirt from a dresser drawer, "I can't ravish you again until I feed you, so I'm going to address the oversight."

And then he was gone, padding in his bare feet out to the kitchen. A light flipped on from outside the bedroom, making her realize how dim it had been before. She listened to him opening cabinets and drawers. Dishes and pans dinged against the granite countertop.

She should be flattered he wanted to take care of her this way, and she was. They hadn't eaten in hours, and her stomach growled at the idea of food.

But even as she slid from his bed to find her suite and change, April wondered if by sleeping with him she'd made a mistake she couldn't recover from. He was related to her case, and she would have to formally disclose her relationship with him to her boss. That was a professional line she'd never crossed, and that was only the beginning of her misgivings about being with Weston.

What concerned her more was how tender she felt in the aftermath. Not just her body, although her lips were swollen from kissing and a few places felt the sweet abrasion of a whisker burn. There was a rawness in her chest that made her wary. A sensitivity that she had no business feeling after being with him just once.

As she closed the door to her suite behind her and dialed on the shower in the bathroom, she hoped that the hot water would help her recover herself. Because no matter what happened in Montana with Weston this week, she had a life to return to in Denver. A complicated, messy existence vastly different from the one she'd tried on like a new dress while she worked at Mesa Falls Ranch.

It would be tough enough to walk away from this far more glamourous life that Weston inhabited. She couldn't make it any harder on herself by developing an attachment to him that would never survive the real world.

It had been so much more than just sex.

The thought kept returning to Weston's mind, and he kept ignoring it, not ready to think about what had just happened with April. Instead, he breathed in the cooking scents, the earthy sweetness of locally

sourced homemade corn tortillas taking him back
to his childhood in the Sierra Nevada Mountains.
The tortillas he rolled now hadn't been made by his
abuela Rosa, like the ones of his youth, but the hint
of corn was fragrant enough to transport him to his
grandmother's kitchen just the same.

He'd only recently discovered a joy in cooking of
all things, an interest his father would surely rank
with basket weaving for its usefulness to a rancher's life. But ranching was only one step in putting
food on a table. Cooking came next. And something
about the sensory experience of chopping and dicing,
sautéing and simmering, helped to settle his thoughts
when they were churning too fast. Like now, in the
aftermath of that incredible encounter with April. He
needed a distraction to keep him grounded. Prevent
him from overthinking everything that was happening between him and the sexy financial forensics
investigator.

Covering the enchiladas in the skillet, he set the
small table in the breakfast nook for them. He liked
the proximity to the big stone fireplace that was open
on one side to the living room and on the other to
the kitchen.

Hearing the subtle shudder of pipes that meant the
water was being shut off in the guest bath, Weston
found his thoughts turning back to April. Straightening the white stoneware plate on its woven gray
place mat, he tried not to think about her stepping
naked out of the shower.

He failed spectacularly.

Damn, but she was breathtaking.

He'd never lost himself so thoroughly being with a woman, and it rattled him. He needed to stay focused on protecting Mesa Falls Ranch from whatever fresh hell was going to rain down on them once April closed her case. Not just for himself, but for all the owners, who had invested more than just their income in the property. The six of them had bought into a dream when they'd purchased the land and turned it into a profitable working ranch. The place wasn't some sentimental way to remember Zach, although that had been part of it at the beginning.

It was a means of giving back. A way to live with the guilt that came from being successful in the world when Zach had lost the chance to become the man he was destined to be. Mesa Falls Ranch was a model of green ranching and land management. The property showcased responsible grazing techniques that resulted in a better ecosystem and healthier environment. They'd poured in capital to do things the right way, and now they were investing in marketing initiatives to inspire and educate.

Not because any of them were inherently altruistic guys. But because Zach's memory had become their social conscience. And Weston would do anything necessary to protect that.

Thinking about his fellow owners, he remembered that Gage had texted him while he was at Fallon's earlier. He'd been so preoccupied with April at the time he hadn't checked the message. He pulled his phone from his back pocket and slid the case onto the kitchen counter, scrolling through his notifications. Finding the text from a few hours ago, he double clicked to open the window.

Tabloid reporter left two messages asking for comment on what Alonzo was like as teacher/friend. I have not returned calls, but most recent voice mail implied she's going to visit Mesa Falls. Call me.

Shit.

Weston stabbed the phone icon to connect with Gage. His friend picked up on the first ring.

"We've got a situation here, Rivera," he said without preamble. There was some noise behind him that sounded like an evening news broadcast before the volume lowered and was quiet. "We need to meet."

"Because of this reporter?" Weston listened for sounds from the guest suite. For now, April's door remained closed.

Not that his call was a secret, but he didn't want to seem inattentive. He regretted leaving their bed so quickly, but he'd wanted to make her dinner.

"She called Desmond and your brother too," Gage informed him, referring to Desmond Pierce, a casino resort owner who held a stake in Mesa Falls. "She hasn't contacted you?"

"What's the name?"

"Elena." Gage cursed softly. "Why the hell didn't

you answer me sooner? We need to get on top of this."

Weston bit down the urge to remind him he'd tried to tell Gage the same thing the day before in regard to April. And where had he heard that reporter's name before? Elena sounded familiar.

"I'm aware of that," Weston said simply, giving the sauce a stir before returning the lid to the skillet. "Might I remind you I'm handling our other PR crisis in the form of the financial investigator?" Guilt rose at his divided alliances, his gaze returning to the guest suite door.

Still closed.

"Right." Gage paused a moment, and Weston could hear ice cubes clinking like he was taking a drink. "How's that going? Is she finding out anything?"

"We're in Kalispell to interview Aunt Fallon."

It took Gage an extra second to reply. "We?"

He ground his teeth together.

"Yes, damn it. We can't afford to have the backlash from Alonzo catch us unaware." He paced away from the range into the living area to distance himself from the guest suite, knowing April would be out soon. "So do me a favor and manage the reporter for me while I keep an eye on things here."

"That's just the problem," Gage shot back. "Elena is about to be your problem too. I'm staring at an Instagram profile for Elena Rollins, and it shows her at LAX with a ticket to Missoula in her hand and a promise to her fans that she's 'tracking a scoop.'"

The muscles in Weston's shoulders knotted so tight he had to knead one with his free hand. "Then someone else needs to come to the ranch and run interference." He paced around the living room, trying to loosen the muscle as a dull ache thudded in his head. "I can't put out all the fires when we've got threats coming from every side since Tabitha Barnes decided to unmask Alonzo in front of the cameras."

"I'm calling a meeting. On-site." Gage's words surprised him. The investors rarely got together, preferring to leave operations to Weston.

Perhaps preferring to forget about the past they shared too.

"When were you thinking?" Weston knew he ought to be grateful that the other owners were going to finally put their heads together about the Alonzo Salazar mess. But part of him resented the intrusion on what little time he had left with April before she closed her investigation.

"This weekend. I've got a new public relations director I can tap to put together an event on short notice. Something to deflect public attention from scandalmongers, or at the very least, make the trip serve a good cause."

Gage assured Weston he'd get back to him with more details soon, and they hung up just as the door to the guest suite opened. Weston shoved his phone in his pocket and returned to the kitchen.

"Whatever you're cooking smells fantastic." April's voice chased away some of the tension in his shoulders, but his conversation with Gage reminded him how much was at stake for the Mesa Falls owners if the Alonzo Salazar scandal tainted their work with the ranch.

He needed to stay on top of her investigation.

She padded into the kitchen in a long-sleeved white T-shirt and blue plaid flannel pajama pants, stopping near the range. Her long hair was still damp and clipped in a haphazard knot. She breathed in the fragrant tortillas from her position near the cooktop.

She was even lovelier with no makeup, the high color in her cheeks an aftereffect of the shower. His hands itched to wrap around her curves and haul her close. But he needed to keep things light. Easy. Temporary.

"I hope you like it." He placed a silver water pitcher on the table and then returned to the stove, lifting the lid so she could see what was inside. "My go-to dishes are the foods of my youth. Mexican and Latin inspired."

Steam wafted up, sending his thoughts back to the shower she'd taken alone. The opportunity he'd missed, damn it.

"I've never tried to cook anything remotely resembling Mexican food, but I love to eat it when I go out." Setting down the spare fork, she retrieved a spatula from a tin on the counter. "Would you like me to help serve? Not that I'm starving or anything."

He laughed as he took the spatula from her, appreciating the lighter moment. "Feel free to choose a wine if you want one, and I'll serve us." He pointed to the door of the under-cabinet wine fridge. "I'm relieved to hear you brought your appetite."

"Relieved?" She bypassed the wine and moved toward the table in the breakfast nook, pausing by the stone hearth to warm her hands.

"I've been out here really questioning my life choices when I heard you showering alone while I opted to cook." He did a poor job of hiding the hunger from his voice. "But I'm glad to feed you."

After sliding the enchiladas onto beds of spinach and greens, he brought the plates of food to the table.

Her gaze followed him. He felt it well before he allowed himself to meet her eyes, which wasn't until he slid into the bench seat next to her, knee grazing hers. The scent of her hair—like winter spices—drifted toward him along with the more subtle, unique fragrance of her skin. He couldn't stop himself from skimming a hand along her thigh, letting it rest on the soft flannel.

"For what it's worth—" her voice held a husky note "—I'm not opposed to multiple showers in a day."

Need for her clamored inside him all over again, but he kept it in check. He tipped her face up to his, limiting himself to a kiss.

"In that case," he murmured over her lips, lingering there, "you'd better eat to keep your strength up."

Pulling away with an effort, he watched her as she took her first bite.

She closed her eyes for a moment, her small hum of pleasure sending a wicked thrill through him. "It's delicious."

"Glad you like it." He dug into his own meal to keep himself from kissing her again. He just needed to find a way to balance the benefits of being with her, to give them the chance to let their passion run its course. A way to keep things uncomplicated.

One of the reasons he'd gotten close to her in the first place was to keep tabs on her investigation. To be aware if she unearthed anything potentially damaging on Alonzo Salazar that could come back to haunt the Mesa Falls Ranch owners. That need hadn't gone away. If anything, it was more important than ever as she closed in on answers.

Biding his time, he let her enjoy her dinner while he debated how to broach the subject tactfully. He filled their water glasses from the pitcher, the flames from the fireplace reflecting on the silver urn.

"You didn't say much about the visit with Fallon on our way back here tonight." He knew they'd both been thinking about being together. Desire had built so high it had drowned out everything else. "Did she have much to offer on Alonzo?"

April nodded. "It was well worth the trip to see all of the postcards he sent her. I'd heard from multiple sources that he traveled frequently, but not even his sons knew where he went. If he was doing humanitarian work like Fallon suggests, then I don't know why he would have been secretive about it."

"So you think that's not the case? That he lied to Fallon about building houses in poor cities around the globe?" Defensiveness rose up in him. He knew damned well those photos weren't faked. "My aunt went on some of the trips, you know."

"I'm not suggesting he was lying." She glanced up from her plate, no doubt hearing the wariness in his voice. "It will be very easy to find out more about his travel now that I have a clue where to begin. I'm just wondering if he had other agendas while he traveled. No doubt he researched the Argentina setting of *Hollywood Newlyweds* on one of those trips."

Weston hadn't given the book much thought since the revelation that author A. J. Sorensen had in fact been Weston's old mentor. But obviously, there was public interest in the story if that tabloid reporter was on her way to Montana. Would reporters be able to dig up information April didn't have access to? No doubt tabloid journalists wouldn't be bound by the same ethics as April. Yet Weston guessed she would discover the truth in the end. She was relentless in her quest to make the pieces add up, a fact that made him both proud and wary, considering he couldn't afford for the details he'd shared with her from his past to come to light. That horseback-riding trip had been life changing for every single one of the ranch owners. And their secrets weren't his to share.

But right now, April herself was the more interesting mystery, as far as he was concerned. Curiosity about her made him interested in her work on a personal level too.

"So now you'll investigate what he did while he was abroad?" he asked, trying to follow the course she was taking through her case.

"Yes." She twirled her fork through a strand of cheese. "But I have support staff in Denver that can do the legwork. I submitted dates and place data to them, and they will use our resources to see what they can unearth. While I wait to hear back—"

"You already did that?" Weston couldn't imagine when she'd found time. Maybe she would stay a step ahead of the tabloids.

"My client is devoting considerable resources to finding answers that have already taken me too long to unearth." The slight furrow in her brow revealed her frustration about that. And, of course, she didn't need to remind him that he'd thwarted her for weeks when she'd tried to learn more about Alonzo. "I sent the information I collected from my phone while you were stocking Fallon's hearth."

It was an important reminder that she was working all the time, and that she didn't owe her first loyalty to him. She wouldn't hesitate to pass along whatever she learned to her client, Alonzo's son. Weston should have asked her about it sooner.

He'd seen her on her phone, of course, but hadn't realized she'd acquired so much from her brief conversation with his aunt. "Good," he said belatedly.

"I'm going to see what else I can find out about Nicole Smith and her mystery nephew. There are no records for them under those names, but I can look for them other ways until I can speak to her again." She lifted her water glass for a sip, watching him over the rim.

"How?" As soon as he asked, he realized he probably had no right to know. "That is, only if you're able to tell me. But if that's too close to the case to answer—"

"It's no secret," she assured him, setting her glass back on the table and shifting in her seat so she could see him better. There was a hint of excitement in her voice, as if she looked forward to finding those final answers for her case. "Most of what I do involves searching databases the public has access to anyhow. My next step in this instance is to review birth records from hospitals closest to Dowdon from thirteen years ago. Cross-check the Matthews just in case the first name is real."

"Makes sense," he said, trying to come up with worst-case scenarios for why Alonzo would have been hiding income. And—if the lead about him supporting a child was true—why would he try to hide his support of the boy?

More importantly to Weston, how might those reasons affect Mesa Falls? Already the publicity from the Christmas gala had taken a less-than-glowing turn. Once Tabitha Barnes dropped the bombshell about Alonzo's authorship of *Hollywood*

Newlyweds, social media about the ranch had been focused on the gossip instead of the green ranching initiatives.

If anything, the money they'd poured into publicity had only magnified the public's attention on the Alonzo Salazar mystery, fueling gossip. Normally, he would never follow that kind of thing.

Now, he didn't have a choice.

"I know you're concerned about how this case will affect Mesa Falls Ranch." April surprised him by latching on to his thoughts. She set down her fork with a gentle clank against the china, meeting his gaze head-on. "But I still haven't figured out why it would."

She pursed her lips for a moment before continuing. "Are you sure there isn't anything you want to tell me—about Alonzo, or about your relationship with him—before the truth comes to light?"

Nine

Weston's square jaw flexed, his shoulders visibly tensing.

April could tell she'd offended him, and she regretted her question. The flames in the hearth danced higher in the silence that followed.

"I'm sorry." She hastened to explain, wanting to smooth things over with the man who'd cooked her dinner and been the most generous lover she'd ever known. He deserved better. "That didn't come out the way I meant it. I'm probably tired from the long days on this case, and that's why I'm not expressing myself well."

His tone was noticeably cooler. "How *did* you mean it?"

"I just have the sense that I'm missing a bigger picture here, since I still don't understand Alonzo's role in the lives of the ranch owners once you left school." She rushed on, trying to pinpoint what bothered her. "He was a mentor during your teens. I get that. But what drew him to Montana for years afterward? I feel like there's an element of the bond between you all that I'm not understanding. Take your brother, for instance."

Weston scowled and shook his head, as if the mere mention of his brother was enough to make him want to end the conversation. "What would my family have to do with any of this?"

"Miles Rivera is one of the ranch owners." April had done her homework on the Mesa Falls organization back when she'd been looking for clues about Alonzo's frequent trips there. "From what Fallon said, the two of you must not have much in common outside of that."

Weston exhaled a long breath and pushed back from the table, closing his eyes for a moment.

"Miles and I are eleven months apart in age. That put us in the same class at school, and he survived the horseback trip from hell along with the rest of us. That's a far stronger bond between us than our blood tie." His hand resting on the bench seat between them clenched and then relaxed again.

She waited, thinking Weston was turning out to be more difficult to understand than her case.

"And frankly, I don't feel like it's my place to discuss the other ranch owners with you." He rose to start clearing their plates, and she stood to help. "But if you want to know more about them—my brother included—I can arrange for you to meet them."

He set a stack of dishes on the counter while she began filling the dishwasher.

"Really?" She was surprised by the offer when he'd kept her at arm's length from his business for so long, but she wanted this opportunity. For her work, yes. But she also craved a deeper understanding of him personally. "That is, I would be very grateful for an introduction."

His gaze roamed over her, and his shoulders eased a fraction. "There is a catch."

"What is it?" Her skin heated from his attention, a welcome reminder that their night together hadn't ended yet. No matter how tense their conversation became, there was the possibility of ending it in a smoldering embrace.

If only all of her life obstacles could recede into the background that way.

He wrapped the leftovers and slid the plate into the well-stocked fridge. Turning back toward her, he took her hand and pulled her away from the granite counter.

"No cleaning for you," he explained. "You're my guest."

"But you cooked," she tried to protest, her efforts weakened by the feel of his warm fingers stroking along the hem of her shirt above her hips.

"We're not keeping score," he assured her, his caress working its magic to loosen her limbs and make her body hum with anticipation. "And you deserve more downtime in your life."

His words crept past the boundaries she needed to have with him, touching her emotions. Stealing her thoughts. She struggled to redirect the conversation back to more neutral ground, all the while feeling that chink in her defenses.

"In that case, thank you." Her throat felt dry, and she cleared it, needing to move on. "And you haven't told me the catch yet. How can I meet more of the ranch owners?"

He lowered his head to hers, his warmth seeping into her skin and blocking out her view of anything else. She wanted him again.

Needed him.

How had she given him so much sway over her when they'd known each other such a short amount of time?

"Gage and I spoke while you were in the shower," he admitted. "Apparently there's more tabloid interest in Alonzo, so we're having an investor meeting this weekend. As many of them who can attend will descend on Mesa Falls as soon as possible."

The news stunned her. She straightened to look Weston in the eye, a chill chasing away all the sweet heat from a moment before.

"Having Alonzo's secret life exposed poses that much of a threat that six of the nation's wealthiest men are going to drop everything to fly to Montana at a moment's notice?" She had suspected that Weston must be keeping something significant from her in regard to his former mentor.

This certainly seemed to confirm it.

"It's not that it poses a threat." He let go of her waist, his hands falling to his sides. "But we share a common interest in protecting the name of someone who mentored us. Someone important to us."

"Shouldn't you leave that to my client?" Frustration throbbed in her temple, making her wonder if this relationship had completely clouded her judgment. "Alonzo's son?"

"If we trusted Devon or Marcus Salazar to protect their father's interests, yes. But you have to admit, your client never showed much interest in his old man before Alonzo's death." Weston paced away from her, pausing by the stone fireplace to glare into the flames. "It's telling that Devon had to hire an investigator to find out anything about his father, isn't it? And I know for a fact that Alonzo invited both his sons to the ranch multiple times in the years before he died. Neither of them came until it was too late."

April knew that Alonzo's deathbed wish had been to have his sons visit the ranch after he died. That was when Devon had hired April's firm, after securing papers that his father had left for them with the ranch owners. April didn't know much about that, but from her perspective, it seemed like Devon was doing whatever he could to unravel the mystery of his father's life.

A mystery Weston seemed determined to keep hidden.

Still, she couldn't afford to alienate him now when he'd offered her an entry to his world. Access to his fellow owners who had proven impossible to interview.

"I understand why you would have a hard time trusting Devon." She joined Weston by the stone hearth, where she watched the firelight play over his features. "And I am grateful for the invitation next weekend."

He glanced up, his hazel gaze inscrutable, his hands shoved in the front pockets of his jeans. The waistband rode low on his hips, revealing a glimpse of taut abs just under the hem of his T-shirt, reminding her he wasn't wearing a damned thing under the denim.

She bit back her response to him, focusing on their conversation.

"The meeting place is undecided, but we usually try to coordinate some kind of good works opportunity while we're together." Straightening from his spot at the fireplace, he removed his hands from his pockets and reached for her. "I'll let you know once the venue is determined."

Should she be warier about their relationship now that she suspected he knew more about Alonzo than he was sharing with her? Logically, she would answer yes. But the draw of the man was too potent. And she needed his help if she ever wanted to get to the bottom of where Alonzo's money had really gone. It was a poor excuse for letting her hormones make her decisions for her, but there it was.

"Okay. Thank you." Nodding, she let him pull her against him, her body melting into his in a way that defied description. They fit together perfectly. "And for what it's worth, I'm sorry about the added tabloid attention. I know that has to be frustrating."

The scent of his skin called to her through his T-shirt. She smoothed her palm along his chest, her forehead resting on his jaw.

"Gage said a reporter was promising her followers a story and posting a photo of a plane ticket to Montana." He shook his head, but kept a grip on April's shoulders, holding her close.

"Should we drive back tonight?" She tipped her head up to look at him. "Do you need to be there for potential damage control?"

He cupped her chin with one hand before he kissed her cheek with a lingering brush of his lips.

"I appreciate the offer, but there's no way I'm leaving here yet." He trailed another kiss down her neck, just below her ear.

Shivers chased each other down her spine.

"I don't want you to regret the time here with me if something goes wrong."

He paused to look down at her, his expression serious.

"First of all, there's no way a tabloid journalist is going to be better at getting answers—real answers—than you. I'm not worried she's going to show up and suddenly uncover the truth overnight."

His faith in her work touched her, even as doubts crept in. "But—"

Before she could voice her concerns, he stilled her lips with a kiss. A slow, thorough kiss that scattered her thoughts and reminded her of how incredible he could make her feel. By the time he eased back, her pulse was thrumming fast, her skin tingling with anticipation.

"Besides," he continued, his voice pitched low in her ear, "there is a bed in the other room, and more than anything else, I need you in it."

So much for keeping things light.

But Weston didn't know if he'd ever have time alone with April like this again. Especially when all hell could break loose in Mesa Falls at any moment.

He'd be damned if he was going to hold this woman at arm's length tonight when he wanted her with a fierceness he'd never felt for anyone else.

Her lips worked silently for a moment before she bit the lower one and gave a jerky nod. "I like the way you think."

His body revved at the green light. And even though they'd just been together, he felt all the same urgency as before. More, even. Because now he knew what awaited them. Remembered the way she whispered his name when she found release. Recalled how her whole body trembled when she freed it from all the damnable restraint she exercised the rest of the time.

"Put your arms around my neck," he urged, ready to see that side of her again.

More than ready to bury himself in her sweetness.

She did as he asked, and he hauled her up into his arms, carrying her through the living area back to the bed in the master suite. He wanted to lay her in the middle of the duvet and strip her clothes from her beautiful body, kiss every square inch of her. But she put a hand on his chest before he could settle her there.

"I want to undress you this time." Her splayed fingers curled gently against him, her fingernails lightly raking against the cotton tee. "Do you mind?"

Mind? He only wished he had every lamp on in the room so he could burn the memory of it into his brain.

"I'd like that," he said, setting her on her feet. She landed silently on the gray-and-white rug.

Her blue gaze darted from his shoulders to his hips, as if to assess the situation. The tiny furrow between her brow revealed how much thought she was giving to where to begin. His body throbbed already, anticipation ratcheting up fast.

When her attention returned to his eyes, a sexy grin plucked at the corner of her mouth. "I may have fantasized about doing this that night we spent on Trapper Peak."

Her fingertips slid beneath the hem of his T-shirt, skating over his skin with a tentative touch. He braced himself for her exploration, only too glad to be her fantasy.

"I wouldn't have complained." Not even subzero temperatures could cool a heat like this.

She skimmed the T-shirt up his back, and he lifted his arms to help her tug it off. Then she shrugged out of her long-sleeved thermal, tossing it aside to rest on top of his discarded shirt.

His gaze snagged on the sight of her breasts swelling above white lace cups, an embroidered red rose nestled between, and he couldn't see anything else. She looked impossibly beautiful in the muted glow from the lamp above a painting near his bed. Her gaze tracked her fingertips as she smoothed them along the exposed skin just above his jeans, the denim all but shrink-wrapping him, getting more and more uncomfortable the longer she wielded those barely there touches.

She leaned closer to press a kiss to the base of his throat, her breasts straining the white lace of her bra with the movement, her breath coming faster. And still he let her set the pace, even now that he was twitching to be inside her. When she eased his zipper down—oh, so carefully—he knew his control was slipping. Fading.

Flinging off his jeans, he left her long enough to

find a condom, his blood pounding so hard he felt light-headed. He returned to the bedroom to see her sidle out of her pajama bottoms, a tiny patch of white lace covering the V between her thighs. He told himself not to fall on her like a starving man, but the truth was he needed her.

Now.

He ripped open the condom packet and sheathed himself before he even reached the bed. Dropping to the edge of the mattress, he pulled her down with him. She straddled him, those luscious breasts of hers grazing his chest and making him realize he hadn't undressed her yet. Somewhere in the back of his brain he was appalled to make rookie mistakes with her, but being with April was so damned different than any other woman it didn't even matter.

He was about to peel off the last of her clothes when she curved a palm around his hard length, stroking him from base to tip. He couldn't think. Could barely breathe.

Instead, he listened to her breath, ragged and rasping. In. Out. Her lips fastened to his throat, her tongue licking him while she positioned herself over him, sliding her lace underwear to one side.

His hips jerked, and he was already pushing inside her. She felt so. Damned. Good.

Sensation surged through him. Wrecked him. He anchored her waist with one arm, guiding her into the rhythm he wanted, hoping like hell she was as close as he was. He moved slowly, trying to give her time, listening to find out what she liked best.

When she began to make kittenish moans, he sped up. He kissed the soft swell of her breasts, lingering over a taut nipple that spilled out of the lace. Her fingernails bit into his shoulders, her thighs clamping against his, and then her release was upon her. Her body squeezed his, urging him on even though he didn't need any encouragement. He came so hard the pleasure mingled with pain in the best possible way. Stealing all his breath. Wrenching through every muscle.

He wrapped her in his arms afterward. Wordless and sated. He pulled a woven blanket over them both and stroked her silky waves, the perfect curls having given way to tousled bedhead that invited his touch. She fit against him like she was made to be there, her breath huffing softly against his chest.

He knew it couldn't last. Not this perfect night together. Not the connection they felt.

But for now it didn't matter. Nothing mattered except that she was here in his arms. She wasn't here because of her case or because she wanted to get close to one of the wealthy owners of Mesa Falls Ranch. April was here because she felt the same irresistible draw that he did.

That would have seemed like a miracle. Two people drawn together because they both felt the magnitude of inevitability. An undeniable attraction.

But it wasn't a miracle, because it would come to

an end. Once the investor meeting was done and she had all the answers she wanted, she would go back to Denver. She'd return to her mission of making numbers add up, bringing order to a messy world one financial investigation at a time.

As for him? He would fulfill the promises of his past, honoring the friend he couldn't save by ensuring good works were done in his name. He'd protect the rest of his friends, who each had his own reasons for not wanting the past to come to light. Somehow, he would keep the scandalmongers of the world at bay while he did it.

He only hoped that his inevitable parting with April would be peaceful. Because if her need for answers threatened the remaining secrets he had to keep, the perfect harmony he felt at this moment wouldn't end simply.

Their whole relationship would implode. And no matter how much he cared for this incredible woman falling asleep beside him, he couldn't afford to be the one who was burned.

Ten

The return to Mesa Falls Ranch felt like a fall from paradise after the idyllic night spent with Weston.

Taking shelter from the world in her accommodations at the main lodge two days afterward, April scrolled through emails in an in-box crammed full of messages about her case. She'd had no luck tracking down a Matthew Smith born at hospitals near Dowdon but had received a list of other boys named Matthew born within a forty-mile radius during that year, as well as new travel records for Alonzo. She had all sorts of developments to comb through, which had forced her to decline Weston's offer to meet him for dinner that evening.

She knew he faced a lot of work of his own today

since a tabloid reporter was apparently already staking out the ranch for a story. But even with the increasing social media interest in Mesa Falls, Weston had made time for April tonight, inviting her to his home for dinner.

Yet she'd forced herself to stay in her room. Alone.

A decision she was beginning to regret now that bedtime neared and she'd only eaten a protein bar for supper. A decision she'd regretted long before that, actually, since she craved seeing Weston again far more than she wanted food. But she couldn't allow her need for him to overrule her work ethic. She wasn't on vacation, after all. She'd been glued to her phone for hours, trying to make sense of the myriad results she'd received from the staff back at her home office in Denver. All of which would have been more rewarding if she'd been eager to close her investigation. But now that she was developing feelings for Weston?

She definitely didn't have the same drive to wrap things up in Montana just to return to her mother's problems. And when she left, her own life would seem even more lonely than before she'd met the most compelling man she'd ever known. Staring blankly at the data on her screen—a travel log with confirmed dates and airfare for Alonzo Salazar's travels—she wondered if it had been a mistake to make that trip to Kalispell with Weston in the first place. She'd hoped maybe the passion between them would burn out if she let it blaze, hot and fast.

Instead, her time with him had only deepened the bond between them. He was so much more than an attractive man. She'd gotten to see his tender thoughtfulness toward his aunt. She'd experienced his generosity as a lover. And she couldn't forget his support of her work by bringing her to meet Fallon Reed in the first place. On top of all she already knew about him—that he would even hike into the snowy peaks of western Montana to save her—she knew she was in over her head. How much deeper would she fall once she attended the investor meeting with him next weekend?

As his date.

Reaching for the refillable water bottle she kept on her nightstand, she unscrewed the cap and tried to focus on her work, since ruminating about Weston only made her chest ache. Her gaze moved from the travel log on her screen to an incoming message from Nicole Smith. She clicked on it right away, since Nicole hadn't responded to her text the day before.

I got fired yesterday before I boarded the plane to return to Mesa Falls Ranch with the rest of my co-workers. I was told my belongings would be shipped to me and that I would be escorted from the premises if I return. Know anything about that?

The message was accompanied by a red-faced emoticon with steam coming from its ears.

April went back and reread the text. Twice.

Was Nicole implying that April had somehow gotten her fired? Worse, had she—inadvertently—done just that by discussing Nicole's presence at Mesa Falls with Weston? She didn't want to think that he'd orchestrated something like that without her knowledge, but then again, he'd made it clear that he had secrets to keep that weren't his own. What if he'd fired Nicole to protect the other ranch owners?

Wariness and worry mingled, making her wonder if she'd been wrong to trust him with as much information as she had about her investigation.

Biting her lip, she debated how to respond, knowing that Nicole was crucial to the case in spite of the fact that she still hadn't provided April with any concrete evidence of funds dispersed to her nephew through a channel that April could trace. She'd sent some bank statements to show regular deposits, but without knowing where the money came from, that information was worthless. So she typed her reply.

I didn't know anything about it. I hope the circumstances won't prevent a conference call at your convenience. We will learn more together than separately.

Slipping from the bed where she'd been propped with her laptop for hours, April wandered to her window overlooking the snow-covered grounds. In the distance, she could see the small pond with its skaters and the lodge where she'd first kissed Weston over dinner. Between the lodge and the pond, a few lighted paths glowed eerily, the low landscape lighting covered with fresh snowfall so that the very earth seemed to glow bright white.

She loved the clean look of the guest ranch. There was no clutter or excess decoration. Just beautiful nature and well-structured buildings. Lights to ensure the place remained easy to navigate even at night. Somewhere out there, Weston Rivera had a house high above the Bitterroot River, half built into a mountainside. She'd heard about it but hadn't seen it with her own eyes. She wondered if he was there now, thinking of her. Missing her.

Or was she just ten kinds of foolish for feeling something for him after what they'd shared?

She wondered how she could continue to avoid him all week until the investor meeting. As if that would prevent her from falling for him.

She feared she was only delaying the inevitable.

Her phone chimed again. She hoped it might be Weston firming up a time for the event he'd promised she could attend. But it was Nicole again.

There was no message in the body of the text.

Just an attachment.

April clicked on it and saw that it was a bank deposit detail that included lines for both the payer and payee. The payee had been carefully blocked out, presumably by Nicole to keep her sister's identity secret a little longer. The payer was still legible, however. A limited liability corporation called Clear-Skies, all one word.

April didn't need to review her notes to recall ClearSkies was a shell corporation used by the nominee service that Alonzo Salazar employed to handle the income from his book. That nominee service allowed Salazar to conduct business without his name being used. He'd paid taxes through the lawyers and covered his travel expenses using checks from Clear-Skies.

Now the connection between Alonzo and Nicole Smith's nephew was clear. She held the proof in her hands. The evidence, in conjunction with the way Nicole had just been fired from her position, suggested that someone in a position of power at Mesa Falls didn't want the connection coming to light. Was Nicole's nephew one of the secrets the ranch owners were keeping?

Frustration simmered through her at the thought.

She didn't know if Weston had been the one to personally fire Nicole, but she suspected he'd had a hand in it after April had shared her progress on the case and Nicole's involvement. If he'd shared that information with the other owners, she might have inadvertently thwarted her own case.

Her exhaustion retreated as adrenaline took over. She slid her feet into a pair of boots and shoved her arms into the sleeves of her warmest coat. She would find Weston tonight and get to the bottom of it, one way or another.

Because no matter what feelings she'd developed for him, her case had to come first. If he was going to share her confidences, she would remind him that she could also share his. She wouldn't even have far to look to find a way to deliver on that.

Even now, a tabloid reporter hungry for a story was due to check into the ranch any minute.

Elena Rollins was here to kick ass and take names.

At least, that was the mantra she kept repeating to herself as she dragged her battered suitcase with a broken wheel along the icy path from the parking lot.

A Southern California girl at heart, she had no clothes appropriate for Montana. A newly destitute girl, thanks to the world's worst divorce, she was lucky to have as many clothes as she still did.

Her ex-husband's new girlfriend had moved in while Elena was at a work conference tracking makeup trends for her Instagram in her former career as a beauty influencer. While Elena had been building her following to help her eventually work from home to have the kids her ex supposedly wanted, her replacement was busy laying claim to all of Elena's things in her LA residence. When she'd returned, she'd been forced to start from scratch.

Elena's high heels didn't fare any better on the ice than her suitcase with the broken wheel. They both thumped, out of sync, as she approached the main lodge building to check in to a hotel she couldn't afford.

But she wasn't bitter about her ex or his new live-in girlfriend. Much. On some level, she'd always known her marriage to the mild-mannered cooking show host had been a rebound relationship after the one man who'd broken her heart. That was on her. She should have taken her time to heal after her long-ago breakup with Gage Striker, one of the owners of Mesa Falls Ranch. If she'd done that in the first place, she never would have married her ex.

So maybe the time had come to deal with her past. This tabloid story she planned to write would stir trouble for Gage, and she couldn't deny taking a small bit of pleasure in that. Elena would gladly bankrupt herself for the chance to exact some small payback on Gage, who was at the cause of so many other problems for her.

After the year she'd had, who could blame her for having less-than-charitable thoughts? She'd spent too much of her life being a doormat. Now? She planned to be the one doing the stomping.

Her vision hazy with exhaustion from the flight delays, she almost ran into a picture-perfect blonde dressed in an on-trend trench coat and leather boots. The kind of woman Elena would have once tried to photograph for her "Woman on the Street" posts about beauty. But these days, Elena didn't have the resources to keep up her work as an influencer. She'd been forced to take a temporary gig as an "entertainment journalist" just to make ends meet. The only bright spot in that was getting to write a piece about Gage.

"Excuse me," the blonde blurted, even though it had almost assuredly been Elena's fault for listing sideways with her broken suitcase.

Elena paused to watch the woman hurry toward the row of all-terrain vehicles parked near the lodge. Sliding into the closest one, which looked sort of like a golf cart with tricked-out wheels, the blonde revved the engine and flipped on the headlight, roaring away into the snow.

Talk about badass.

Putting her feet in gear again as she pushed through the double doors of the lodge, Elena promised herself to check one of the vehicles out after she'd had time to catch up on some sleep. Her story would have to wait another day while she got her bearings in Montana and, hopefully, found some clothes suitable for the snow. Her social media following was still large, but she couldn't afford to lose followers with sloppy clothes and poorly thought-out posts. Her following and connections had helped her land this job in the first place, and one day she hoped to return to her old job.

Besides, she needed to publicly chronicle her story as she pursued it. She wanted the Mesa Falls Ranch owners to know she was coming for them. Or, more accurately, she wanted Gage Striker to know she was coming for him, since his betrayal had sent her life on the trajectory that landed her in her unhappy marriage.

Her fault, yes. But Gage bore some blame too. Breaking this story and revealing the secrets of Mesa Falls would not only help her pay the bills, it would give her a bit of sweet revenge.

Weston scaled a fifty-five-degree bouldering wall in his home gym, trying to work off the frustration brewing inside him ever since April had refused his dinner invitation.

Scratch that.

The frustration had been building before that, when she'd evaded his calls earlier in the day, texting him that she was swamped with work. Swiping sweat away from his eyebrow, he focused on reaching a hold high over his head. Granted, it was hypocritical of him to be upset with her for keeping him at arm's length when he'd known things were temporary between them. Hadn't he already thought about how to keep things amiable when they said goodbye?

Turns out, he sucked at this no-strings kind of relationship. The women in his past tended to be hookups. And April was about as far from a hookup as he could imagine. He liked her—respected her—too much. No matter what his brain told him about keeping things light, he wanted to be with her while she was still in Montana. As far as he was concerned, their time together wasn't over yet.

But it seemed like she believed otherwise.

"Excuse me? Mr. Rivera?" A man's voice from below surprised him.

He peered down from his precarious foothold to see Cedric, his recently hired personal assistant, looking decidedly uneasy. The guy was whip smart, just out of college and dressed like a million bucks. Weston hadn't figured out why he had no self-confidence to go with it, but Cedric hadn't batted an eye at the idea of helping Weston manage a financial empire from a Montana ranch, so Weston liked him well enough.

Except when he interrupted a challenging climb.

"I'm sort of in the middle of something here." The muscles in his right arm shook from the strain of too long a reach.

He turned his attention back to the wall, needing to maintain his focus. A decisive tapping of shoes on tile almost made him look back down, but he fought the urge to solve Cedric's problems for him. The guy needed to learn how to navigate Weston's world on his own.

"Weston?" April's unmistakable soft voice held a steely note as she called up to him. "We need to talk."

A quick glance over his shoulder let him see her hands-on-hips, no-nonsense posture. The fire in her eyes was clearly visible from his semi-inverted position two stories over her head.

No wonder Cedric had been uneasy. She looked like she meant business. Which couldn't be good for Weston.

"Of course," he told her mildly, feeling his way downward. His climb would have to wait. "Cedric, can you see if our guest needs anything before you go?"

He heard the two exchange a few words before his assistant disappeared as silently as he'd arrived, leaving Weston alone in the gym with April. The subterranean room was built into the mountainside along with the rest of Weston's modern home that overlooked the Bitterroot River Valley. He'd spent a lot of time in Mesa Falls during the last two years, but not much in the house itself. If he wasn't working on the ranch, he was joining search-and-rescue efforts on the mountain. Sitting still had never been his thing.

"Is there anything I can do to help?" April asked as he picked his way around an obstacle.

"No," he assured her. "I prefer not to jump until I'm closer to ground level. Easier on the knees."

"I wouldn't expect you to jump," she retorted. "It just didn't occur to me that you'd have to climb back down. At a training facility near me we have ropes to slide down afterward, but then I realized you don't even have a safety harness."

"This is a home gym, and I don't climb for a thrill." Finding the last foothold on the lower side of the rock obstacle, he readjusted his finger hold and then let go.

Falling.

He landed on both feet a few yards from where

she hovered near the punching bag he kept in one corner of the gym.

"I do it to stay in shape for rescues on the mountain. And it's a great workout." He grabbed a towel from the weight bench and mopped his forehead, his muscles still thrumming from the climb and the weight lifting before that.

In fact, he'd been working out for well over an hour in an effort to forget that this very woman hadn't wanted to see him tonight. She looked beautiful in her long trench coat and high leather boots, her hair in smooth curls again. Not like when they'd spent the night together and he'd combed his fingers through it over and over.

Damn, but he'd wanted to end this day with her in his bed again.

She pursed her lips in a look he'd come to know well in the short time they'd been acquainted. She wasn't a woman to blurt out anything, picking over her words before she spoke.

He waited, even though he had the feeling he wasn't going to like whatever she'd come here to say. He would have far preferred to kiss her than listen, but he knew that would only delay the inevitable.

"I didn't realize it was quite this late when I decided to come over here."

"I'm surprised you knew where to find me." His house was far from the main lodge on the guest ranch portion of the property. Tucked into the mountainside, he wasn't close to the working ranch portion of

Mesa Falls, either, since the land here was too rocky and precarious for cattle.

"I stopped by the ranch manager's office to ask Cooper Adler for directions," she admitted. Cooper had been the ranch manager at Mesa Falls even before Weston and his friends had purchased the property. "I needed to speak to you in person. Gauge your reaction for myself."

"About what?" Wary, he braced himself for whatever new information she'd unearthed in her investigation.

"I heard from Nicole earlier this evening." She watched him closely, her gaze narrowing slightly. "She was in LA for three days at the cattle-raising expo."

"I remember." April had told him about that. She'd been anxious to speak to the woman when she returned. "Did you find out her real name? Or her sister's?"

"Not yet." Her blue eyes never wavered from his. "I learned Nicole was fired from her job here. Her employment was terminated while she was still on the tarmac in Los Angeles. It was made clear to her that she won't be allowed on the premises again."

"Fired?" He could tell that April was upset about this, but he wasn't quite sure why she'd want to see his reaction to the news. "You think she was dismissed unfairly? I can look into her performance if—"

Even as he spoke, the pieces fell into place. Something about the skeptical tilt of April's head finally clued him in to what she was thinking.

"You think *I* had something to do with her being let go?" He gripped the ends of the towel he'd draped around his neck, pulling taut.

"Did you?" she asked him point blank.

"Of course not. I didn't know a damned thing about it." He hated that these were the circumstances that had brought her to his place, and not a desire to see him. "I'm trying to help you find the answers you need, April. I don't care if you talk to Nicole."

Some of the tension left her shoulders, making him realize that she really had believed he might have orchestrated an underhanded move like that. On the flip side, her obvious relief at having been wrong told him that he might not be the only one who was starting to care too much.

"Thank you for telling me that." She gave a firm, brief nod, as if her world had been reorganized to her satisfaction. "But my investigator instincts suggest that someone else in a powerful position at Mesa Falls cares very much if I talk to Nicole. Now, more than ever, I think it's important I meet the owners."

He ached with regret that she'd only come here to confront him. And to ensure she still had a chance to meet with his business partners.

"I just got word that we're doing a dinner party at Gage's house Saturday night. Low-key. Just a few environmentally minded celebrities who weren't able to attend the gala before Christmas." The bigger mission of Mesa Falls was spreading awareness of sustainable ranching practices, so the more opportunities they had to showcase that, the better.

"In that case, thank you." She backed up a step as if she was ready to sprint for the door now that she had everything she'd come here for. "I look forward to it."

He clenched the towel tighter in an effort not to haul her against him. He wanted to touch her. Taste her.

But the walls she was putting between them were starting to feel like the kind he couldn't climb.

"Will I see you before the party?" he pressed. If she was backing away from him, he wanted her to at least be clear about it.

"Not unless I wrap up my investigation before then." She hesitated in the archway leading out of the gym, as if she couldn't make up her mind whether to stay or go. "My boss is under a lot of pressure from our client. He expected answers long before now."

Weston suspected that was the truth. But he also felt certain she was more than content to hide behind work so she didn't have to confront what was happening between them. He tried his question another way.

"Tell me this then, April. Would I see you before the party if you didn't have to work?" He forced himself not to chase after her. He wouldn't sway her with touches, no matter how much he wanted to do just that.

She swallowed. Took a deep breath.

"I don't think it would be wise to keep—" she seemed to search for the right words "—seeing each other when we both know the end is imminent."

He wanted to ask her why. Because she cared for him and feared walking away would be difficult? Because her work was bound up with his life? There might be a hundred other reasons, but he didn't want to hear them. He only wanted a chance to be with her one last time.

He wasn't ready to say goodbye.

"Then I'll count myself fortunate you agreed to be my date this weekend," he told her simply, already thinking about ways to make the night special. "Just keep in mind if Saturday is the last chance I'll have to spend time with you, I'm pulling out all the stops to make you change your mind."

Eleven

Late Saturday morning, April tipped her face into the wind off the Bitterroot Mountains, wishing she had better weather to climb one last time before she left Montana for good.

Before dawn, she'd stowed her gear in a backpack and requested a ranch utility vehicle to take her to one of the trailheads for Trapper Peak. But one of the ranch hands had spooked her with the weather report while she was loading up the vehicle, insisting a storm was predicted for noontime. April hadn't wanted to risk getting caught up there again and needing Weston to save her.

Again.

So she'd left her bag at the lodge and settled for

a long walk along the Bitterroot River, where she could at least admire the views. There were wide-open spaces interspersed with gentle slopes and the occasional patch of woods, while the craggy gray peaks jutted in the west. Despite the weather prediction, those high mountaintops looked clear enough to her. Maybe tomorrow she could fit in a final climb. Boots crunching through the snow, she just needed this last moment in the outdoors with space and air around her, so different from the crammed suffocation of her mother's house. She feared it would feel all the more claustrophobic after spending this time with Weston.

He'd shown her a different side to herself. Given her a brief glimpse of the life she might have had if she'd made different choices—of who she might have been if she hadn't hatched the adolescent scheme that initiated her mother's downward spiral. Weston had access to a wealthy world that felt foreign to a woman who had to worry about how long she had before her mother's yard broke the local fire code.

Still, Weston's words had replayed in April's head all week long, a refrain she couldn't stop hearing while she toed a rock into a portion of river that wasn't iced over.

I'm pulling out all the stops to make you change your mind.

She wasn't sure why he'd want to change her mind about ending a relationship they'd both known wouldn't last. But she couldn't afford for her heart to be swayed by whatever he had planned for tonight. It was for his own good. He wouldn't be happy with her in the long run.

A huge bird soared past her, casting enough of a shadow to startle her. Peering up, she saw its white underbelly and dark gray body, the mottled feathers and broad wings helping her identify it as a gyrfalcon, a rare winter resident in this part of the country. Weston had told her Mesa Falls' environmentally friendly ranching was boosting the ecosystem all around, and here was beautiful living proof.

She would miss Montana. And Weston.

Her office had already booked her a ticket to Denver tomorrow in the late afternoon. From her boss's perspective, her case was closed now that she'd tracked the majority of Alonzo Salazar's expenses thanks to Nicole Smith's bank deposit statement. The woman's name was actually Nicole Cruz, a piece of information easy enough to find once April had the other details. Matthew Cruz, her nephew, was in a boarding school on the East Coast, the expensive tuition financed entirely by ClearSkies.

April's investigator instincts weren't satisfied since she'd barely scratched the surface of whatever had happened fourteen years ago to spur Alonzo Salazar to write a book that would finance the child's upbringing. But her job had only been to find out where the money had gone.

Between the travel log she'd pieced together thanks to Fallon Reed, and the tip from Nicole Cruz, she'd accounted for ninety percent of it. The rest, in the eyes of her firm, was incidental.

She headed back toward the lodge, giving herself time to get her game face on for the dinner party tonight. In theory, she could back out now that she didn't need to meet Weston's business partners to solve her case. But she'd been enough of a coward with him already. Besides, truth be told, she needed this last evening with him if only to give her closure on their time together.

And perhaps she was indulging herself a little by attending an event that promised to be posh and glittery. She'd even booked an appointment with a local boutique consultant through guest services who'd agreed to bring some sample dresses to her suite this afternoon. She walked faster on the way back, looking forward to choosing the kind of cocktail gown she'd only have the chance to wear once.

Her own Cinderella moment.

When she arrived at the lodge, she saw a delivery van with the name Hailey's Closet painted in elegant font on the side. The vehicle was parked with the side door slid open, and April spotted a silver rolling rack full of hanging garment bags just inside. A trio of women seemed to be having a tense exchange on the curb.

Could they be here for her dress consultation? Checking her watch, she saw it was now just past noon, and her appointment wasn't until one thirty. But just in case, she approached the trio, recognizing one of them as Lorelle, the guest services liaison who'd helped April book her only financial indulgence this trip.

"Excuse me?" She called over to the group as she strode toward them, thinking maybe there was a mix-up with her appointment, or some other issue she could smooth over. "Hi, Lorelle." She greeted the only person she knew, an apple-cheeked matron who frowned down at her clipboard, pen poised over the notes. "Is there a problem with my fitting this afternoon? I'm here now if we need to change the time."

"You're April Stephens?" A younger lady paused her gum smacking to speak to April. She had one lace-up boot on the van's running board while her long, lime-green fingernails gripped the rolling rack. "Could you? There was a mix-up with the times and I can't stay—"

Lorelle scoffed. "*Your* mix-up, not ours. I distinctly told your store manager that I needed two appointments—"

The third woman—a petite bombshell with miles of glossy black waves—interjected. "I'm not sacrificing my time slot. My party is tonight."

April glanced at the beauty with heavy dark eyebrows and sultry voice. April recalled passing her on the way out of the guest lodge the night before when the woman had been swearing colorfully at her suitcase with a broken wheel.

"My party is tonight too," April announced, unwilling to part with her chance to have a special dress on this last evening with Weston.

It would be difficult enough to say goodbye. She at least needed one more memory. One last opportunity to be in his arms. And damn it, she wanted his last vision of her to be one where she looked her best.

Lorelle and the delivery van driver began to bicker again, but the other hotel guest turned wide brown eyes on April.

"Gage Striker's dinner party?" she inquired, arching an eyebrow.

Her face was perfectly heart-shaped, right down to the widow's peak at the center of her forehead. Truly, the woman was so pretty April found it hard to focus on her words. When she dialed in what she'd asked, however, April recalled what Weston said about this evening's get together. Low-key. With a few "environmentally minded celebrities."

The stunner beside her must be someone famous. Faces like hers belonged on TV or the big screen.

"Yes." April smiled warmly, hoping against hope to reason with a fellow partygoer. "Maybe we could share the time slot? Assuming they have both of our sizes on that rolling rack?"

The other woman nodded briskly and turned to the driver.

"Excuse us. Tory? Lorelle?" She gently touched the sleeve of Lorelle's suit jacket. "Ms. Stephens and I have agreed to share the appointment. Tory, do you have samples in both of our sizes in there?"

Lorelle frowned while Tory whooped a delighted "Yes ma'am," and began unloading the rolling rack.

"I'm Elena, by the way," the mystery celebrity said to April as the two of them stepped back to make room on the sidewalk. A bellhop from the main lodge jogged out to help the delivery driver with the clothes. "Could we possibly use your room for a fitting? Mine is a hot mess."

"I'll unlock a suite," Lorelle offered, clearly overhearing them as she stalked toward the huge double doors. "Tory only has an hour." She glared darkly at the driver, who was flirting with the bellhop over the clothes rack. "So follow me, and thank you for being so amenable."

More than satisfied with this solution, April joined the unlikely group as they headed into an elevator cabin. Her phone vibrated in the silence as they were whisked up to the third floor.

She pulled the cell from her jacket pocket just enough to see the caller ID: Mom. Swiping the button to send the call to voice mail, she hoped whatever her mother's latest crisis was, it could wait until tomorrow night, when April would be back home.

For now, she wanted to concentrate on savoring every moment of her last night with Weston. Too bad her heart was already aching at the thought of leaving him.

Maybe Elena's luck was finally turning.

She was riding in an elevator with an actual invitee to Gage Striker's event tonight. The opportunity to learn what she could from April Stephens was too juicy to pass up. Not to mention, spending this time with a legitimate party guest would help give her the details she needed to talk her way in the front door tonight.

Elena was at Mesa Falls Ranch to track the Alonzo Salazar story and sell it to the tabloids, all the while knowing that her long-ago ex-lover was somehow involved since he was one of the reclusive owners of the property.

So far in her discreet inquiries to the staff and outright prying online, she'd learned very little, other than the news that Gage Striker was having a dinner party at his house tonight. All of the ranch owners were expected to be in attendance. She'd immediately started plotting to crash it. To make a devastating, eat-your-heart-out sort of entrance.

And, of course, to film it for her social media channels.

Now she had more than just a vague idea. April Stephens gave her the key to executing the plan.

Elena calculated her approach while Lorelle bustled around the suite, directing Tory's setup of the clothes, pointing out the full-length mirrors and steering Elena and April toward separate bedrooms off the main living area. The guest services coordinator really was doing her best to rectify the appointment snafu, even though the mistake was a godsend for Elena. No doubt they'd get a discount on the clothes she couldn't afford in the first place. And Elena had the chance to discreetly interview April Stephens.

She'd find out whatever she could about why the ranch owners were all flying in to convene on-site. Could it be they were worried about the publicity from the Alonzo Salazar scandal? Publicity she would stir relentlessly after tonight.

It was a lucky day, indeed.

Weston checked his watch as another one of his partners arrived—late—for the afternoon meeting he'd called before tonight's dinner party.

Striding into Weston's media room wearing a crumpled tuxedo that looked like it must have been from a black-tie event the night before, Gage Striker was missing his tie, his French cuffs flapping loose around his wrists. A big, burly New Zealander, Gage had come to the United States to attend Dowdon and never left. Now, he was an angel investor for too many companies to name, and the most unangelic of the group in every other way.

He dropped into one of the leather chairs arranged in two rows before a large screen. Paneled with soundproof tiles and cherry wainscoting, the space was dimly lit. The front row of chairs could be spun around to face the back row, making it easy to talk in here. Weston had ordered food for the meeting, leaving the drinks and sandwiches on the table along one wall in case someone hadn't eaten.

"Finally tore yourself away from your party to join us?" Weston's brother, Miles, asked from the chair beside him.

Miles, of course, had been on time for the meeting. He and Desmond Pierce had shared a flight from the West Coast.

Gage muttered a string of ripe curses before explaining, "I flew home for a family wedding, and I thought I'd better stay as late as I could since I hadn't set foot on Striker land in almost three years. But you know how those flights are. Long, hellish fugues that make you forget what day it is. I slept right through landing."

The ranch had a small landing strip near the river, making it convenient to fly private aircraft almost to their doorstep.

"We might as well get started." Weston sped things along, anxious to tie up business so he could focus on the evening with April. He had flowers scheduled to be delivered to her at intervals all afternoon, but that was just a warm-up for later. He'd put a lot of time and thought into convincing her not to end things for good. "Jonah is stuck in weather and can't be here until the party. Alec had a family emergency."

Jonah Norlander and Alec Jacobsen were the only owners missing from the meeting. Tech company CEO Jonah had a new baby, so his absence wasn't totally unexpected. And game developer Alec's family had always been the most dysfunctional of the group, which was saying something considering the home lives they all came from. Weston wondered if he should have shared more about the Riveras with April, since she seemed to have her hands full with her mother. Hearing about his own issues might have provided some sort of consolation for the stress of being around her mother. But it had been tough enough sharing what he had about Zach when they were in Kalispell. Dumping the family drama on her then had been the very last way he'd wanted to spend their brief time together.

He hadn't realized then that it might be his only window of opportunity.

"How are things with the financial forensics investigator?" Gage asked, blinking his eyes open wider as he straightened in his seat. "How's her case progressing?"

"I won't know until I see her tonight." He'd been shut out while she followed up leads, keeping to herself ever since she'd appeared in his home gym a few nights ago. "But the last time we spoke, she was concerned I'd had one of the staff members fired. Nicole Smith."

He watched his friends' faces to see if any of them showed a trace of recognition. Guilt. But it was impossible to study all three men at once. Gage's expression never shifted, however.

"Why?" Miles asked from Weston's right side, leaning forward to rest his elbows on his knees. "Why would she think that?"

Weston had kept the news to himself this long. Without more evidence that Alonzo was supporting a child with the profits from his book, he wasn't going to point fingers. He'd asked Nicole's supervisor about the termination just the day before, and the woman insisted that it had been a performance-based decision. So maybe April had only imagined there was an underhanded agenda to thwart her case.

"The woman told April she had a tip about the case, but before she could share it, she was fired." Weston shrugged. "Bottom line is that April Stephens keeps her cards close to her vest." She was a professional, and she was good at her job, both qualities he admired about her. "I don't think she's going to leak information publicly, but I know whatever she learns will go straight to Devon Salazar."

"Who we don't trust." Gage leaned back in his chair, threading his hands behind his head as he stretched out. "Neither of Alonzo's sons showed up for him when he needed them."

Alonzo had undergone chemo alone, retreating to the ranch to recover afterward. Neither of his sons had joined him, even though he'd invited them more than once.

"And yet, for all that Alonzo did for us, you have to admit he wasn't much of a father to his own sons." Weston had come to see April's point of view on that, recognizing that Alonzo's secret life had made him seem untrustworthy. "He told us as much."

"So what are you suggesting?" Miles asked,

spearing a hand through his dark blond hair. "That we just hope Devon Salazar keeps Alonzo's secrets?"

The four men in the room remained silent, and Weston guessed they were each contemplating the things that Alonzo had known about each one of them. Their mentor had been the only adult in their lives who'd known what they'd been through. Collectively, with Zach. And, afterward, privately.

The thought of the child Alonzo had allegedly been supporting chirped in Weston's mind again, but he shut it down. He still hadn't seen any proof of the arrangement.

"I'm more worried about the tabloids than Devon," Weston admitted finally. "Elena Rollins checked into the lodge three nights ago, but she hasn't been a visible presence around the property that I can see so far."

"Who?" Desmond asked as he stood from his chair to help himself to the food at the table in the back. He grabbed a plate and started piling meats on a half baguette. "Did I miss something?"

"She's the tabloid reporter," Gage informed him drily, following Desmond long enough to scoop an imported longneck from the bucket. "She also happens to be an ex-girlfriend that my father paid off to ensure nothing tainted my career back when he thought I was going into the family business."

Gage's father was a highly placed politician from a prominent family. He'd paid a fortune for Gage to attend Dowdon and live Stateside with a chaperone year-round, preferring his son's wild-boy antics take place far from their native soil.

Everyone cursed when they heard that the tabloid reporter and Gage had history. "How much does she hate you?" Miles asked after he was done swearing.

Gage grabbed two extra beers and shot him a dark look as he handed drinks to both Weston and Miles.

"That seems like a question that doesn't require an answer."

Nerves knotted in Weston's gut. Not because he had so much to hide himself—he'd been honest with April about the worst of his own past. But for his friends. His partners.

Men he'd move heaven and earth for after what they'd gone through.

Twisting off the cap on his beer, he flipped it into the drink holder built into the arm of the huge home theater chair. What would Zach think of his old crew if he could see them now? Back in school they'd had big dreams of going into business together. Now, it was tough to be together. They were successful, yes. But they were a damned sorry lot in so many other ways when they all found it so painful to set foot on Mesa Falls Ranch, the one business they'd begrudgingly forged together.

Even that had been orchestrated in large part by emails and conference calls. All to avoid feeling the keen sense of loss that being together always stirred.

"So we need a game plan for tonight," Weston reminded his friends, keenly feeling the absence of the one who would never be with them again. "And I'd like for someone else to consider spending more time on site going forward to help me with damage control once the paparazzi start descending on this place."

Every last one of the owners had built a home somewhere on the property when they'd purchased the land, so it wasn't as if they didn't have places to stay. Yet Miles was already shaking his head. Desmond studied the food on his plate. Gage sank into his chair again, crumpling the custom-made tuxedo even more.

"Hell no, mate," he groused. "Not me."

"Ever since Tabitha Barnes unmasked Alonzo in front of reporters at the Christmas gala, we've been on borrowed time keeping the past quiet." Weston curled his fist around the cold beer, wanting to wrap things up so he could move on with his night. With April. "It's all coming to a head. And I'm not going to be standing here alone when it does."

He'd always been content to be the point man for Mesa Falls Ranch business before, but since meeting April, he wanted the opportunity to travel. To woo her. Time apart from her had only made him realize how right they were together. He just needed to find a way to make her believe it too.

"Let's see what tonight brings first, okay?" Desmond suggested as he returned to his seat, sliding his plate onto the stand by his chair while he opened his beer. "We can meet at Gage's house for breakfast in the morning before our flights start leaving. Maybe by then Jonah will be here too, if not Alec."

Nods all around seemed to indicate there was a consensus. They were a hell of a lot quieter group than the boys who'd once torn it up together in school.

Miles cleared his throat and raised his beer. "But for now, thanks, brother, for all you've done here."

Weston felt his eyebrows shoot up into his hairline at his sibling's surprise praise. But it wasn't a bad feeling to see his friends lift their bottles and clink them together, muttering, "Thanks, man," all around.

It was practically a standing ovation, considering the crowd.

Belatedly, he tipped his drink to theirs.

"Always." It was a single simple word, and yet it burned his throat. It was the same word they'd all spoken the night they'd mourned Zach's death and promised to have each other's backs no matter what.

The memory wasn't lost on any of them.

Twelve

"Wow." Weston's greeting made April glad she'd spent the time to find the right dress. "You take my breath away."

His hazel eyes roamed over her with a flare of hot appreciation as they met in the lobby of the main lodge. She'd come downstairs to wait for him, fearing her heart would be too full of emotions if he came to her room, where vases of exotic blooms filled every free stand and table. His over-the-top romantic gesture had touched her even as it gave her a poignant reminder of their vastly different worlds.

Now, she was all the more relieved she'd chosen to meet him down here instead of in the privacy of her room. If they'd been alone, she wasn't sure she'd make it out the door without throwing herself in his arms. Just his gaze on her skin made her warm all over. Meanwhile, as they stood there in the busy lobby, guests mingled and waited for their vehicles from the valet.

"I'm glad you like it." Breathless from his proximity, she peered down at her cocktail gown. She'd chosen the springlike confection in defiance of the snow still on the ground. The sheer, pale green chiffon netting overlaid silk in some places, and bare skin in others, and was dotted with white flowers with tiny seed pearls at their centers. The deep vee of the front and back of the dress flattered her, while the handkerchief hemline teased her calves in soft touches. "I had fun choosing it."

Her impromptu dress consultation with Elena had been more fun than she'd anticipated after the somewhat awkward start. She hadn't wanted to be starstruck while trying on dresses, so she'd refrained from asking about Elena's career, knowing that pinpointing her fame would only make April more nervous. Once Lorelle had left the room, they'd taken turns trying on gowns and giving feedback. Tory, the delivery person, insisted she wasn't a boutique consultant but just a driver, so she hadn't wanted to share her opinion. Instead, she'd spent the time on the phone with her employer, making sure both women received their designer rentals at a fraction of the cost because of the mix-up.

Which made the day all the better, in light of April's finances.

"I hope picking the dress was only the beginning of the fun you're going to have tonight." He took her trench coat from where she'd draped it over her arm.

His words reminded her of all the flowers he'd sent.

"Thank you for the beautiful bouquets, Weston." She hadn't called him to thank him, thinking she'd see him soon enough in person. But after each consecutive delivery—there'd been five—she had felt even more special. "The fragrance in my room is incredible. It will be like sleeping in a hothouse tonight."

His eyes locked on hers as he lifted the coat to drape over her shoulders.

"An image I won't soon forget," he assured her as he moved behind her, carefully sliding her hair to one side in a way that made her back tingle. "You are more than welcome."

With her trench finally settled around her shoulders, the fabric felt like a caress. Or maybe it was just knowing his hands were on the other side of the cloth. A shiver of pleasure tickled its way up her spine at the sight of him in his tuxedo, his hair still damp from his shower.

And then they were heading out of the lodge and onto the carpeted path that led to the valet stand. His Land Rover was already there, headlights on, the engine running. A valet held the passenger side door for her while Weston handed her inside.

When he slid into the driver's seat beside her, she was transported back to their trip to Kalispell, when nerves and anticipation had her thinking about being with him the whole time. Tonight felt sort of the same way, with the electricity buzzing between them. Except for the fact that she already had her ticket home.

A topic she planned to avoid for as long as possible.

"I didn't mention it to you the other night, but your house is really spectacular." There was no other word that felt quite right for Weston's modern home built into a mountainside. "Sort of a feat of engineering, I would think?"

"I hope so." He cracked a smile, his expression shadowed in the dashboard lights as they took an access road through private ranch property. "I have a view of a waterfall right off my deck during the warm months, and a frozen ice cascade the rest of the year. But every spring, it's a little nerve-racking as I wait to see if the ice is going to melt too fast and come crashing through the deck supports."

She laughed lightly. "It comes as no surprise that you are a man who still enjoys living on the edge."

It was one of many things she liked about him. He counterbalanced her need for order, for having her life organized in neat columns. Or maybe she saw in him the kind of life she might have had if she didn't have to be responsible for her mother all the time. If her one attempt to live large and make a statement hadn't led to her mom's illness.

April looked over at his profile. He was quiet so long she wondered if she'd offended him.

"That's not a bad thing," she reminded him. "If everyone played it safe all the time, the world would be a much duller place."

"You can't imagine how much I've reined myself in over the years." He slanted a look at her as he turned onto a steeply pitched road. A four-rail fence ran along either side. "But maybe I've reached a happy medium."

She wanted to ask him more about that, and about the family he didn't seem to feel a part of, but then a three-story log home flanked by a small barn and stables came into view. Clearly, they'd arrived at Gage Striker's home. Landscape lights made the whole place visible even in the dark; the horseshoe-shaped driveway was full of luxury four-wheel drive vehicles dropping off guests in evening attire. A security team worked the area, and a pair of guards was at the front door. Another pair was posted at the corners of the house. Three more were greeting the cars as they neared the house, their presence discreet but visible.

A bout of nerves chilled her as she spotted a celebrity near the red carpet at the front door. She recognized the man from her mother's afternoon soaps, suave and smiling as he helped a pop singer from a black Escalade.

"This must be your dinner party," she said needlessly, telling herself she'd be okay.

If this stunning property was Gage Striker's seasonal home, she could only imagine what his full-time residence must look like. Not that it mattered, April reminded herself. This was her last night with Weston, so she might as well enjoy it.

Prepping for the event with Elena had helped bolster April's confidence for the evening, making her realize how much her mother's illness had chipped away at it over the years. She'd lived so long feeling responsible and embarrassed about her mother's condition that she'd let it stunt her when it wasn't about her.

She hoped the rest of the famous and semifamous guests would be as easygoing as Elena had been.

"It is. Just say the word if you want to be anywhere else in the world," he told her as he put the car in Park near the carpeted walkway. He waved off a liveried attendant before the man could reach the car door. "I'd gladly be your date for whatever you want to do tonight, April. We could fly to New York or Paris if you prefer that kind of thing. Or hell, we could find a mountain range that isn't covered with snow this time of year and take a hike so we can watch the sunrise from a high peak."

The picture he painted took her breath away. She didn't care about Paris or New York. But a hike with him that wasn't about him saving her, or her trying to wrest information from him…the idea touched her. "I wouldn't ask that of you," she half whispered to herself. Unsure.

Besides, a more cynical part of herself reminded her, she'd asked him to introduce her to the other Mesa Falls owners. For all Weston knew, her investigation continued. Was there any chance he didn't want that meeting to take place? The pang of doubt in her chest hurt more than it should have.

"You wouldn't be asking me for something," he replied now, unaware of the dark turn of her thoughts. "I'm asking you what would make you happiest. I just want this time together to be special for you. Perfect."

He reached for her hand and held it between his. The butterflies in her belly relaxed, but a different kind of nervousness returned at the gentle rasp of his callused fingertips against her skin. Her attachment to him had grown too fast. Too deep. Surely no real, lasting feelings could develop for someone that quickly. No matter how she analyzed it, the equation just didn't add up. She couldn't trust a well of emotion she didn't understand.

Taking a deep breath, she forced a smile she didn't quite feel. "Thank you. But I can't wait to meet your friends and get a glimpse of who you are when you're not with me."

She meant it. She did want to understand him better, if only to try to figure out why—how—this man had gotten under her skin in a way no one ever had before. Because now that her case was finished, she didn't need to learn things about the owners of Mesa Falls Ranch. Tonight, she could just try to figure out the man next to her, and what it was about him that captivated her so thoroughly.

"Of course." Weston lifted her fingers to her lips and kissed her knuckles. "In that case, welcome to the party, April. I'm glad to share my world with you."

Her heartbeat stuttered as she looked into his eyes. But then the moment ended too quickly as he raised a hand to wave over the valet. A security officer arrived at Weston's window first, signaling to the valet to wait until they'd been cleared.

Rolling down the vehicle window, Weston passed the man what she guessed was his ID. "Weston Rivera and April Stephens."

The security guard—a woman, April realized now that her face was visible in the light of the dashboard—wore black from head to toe. She wore a padded vest over a heavy thermal jacket and a military-style cap with enough of a brim to cast her face in shadow. There was a hint of a long braid between the cap and her jacket.

"April Stephens?" She repeated the name and pulled out an electronic device smaller than a tablet but larger than a phone. "We show her as having already arrived."

April reached for her purse to show the woman her driver's license, but Weston's hand on hers stilled her.

"Not possible," Weston told the guard smoothly. "April is my guest, and one of my business partners set up your security system for tonight, so I can type in my password if you need it."

The officer's brown eyes shot from her screen to Weston's face. "Of course, Mr. Rivera. My apologies."

She passed him her tablet, allowing Weston to input a password that apparently gave them the green light, because the guard waved them through. When they pulled to a stop, the valet opened the door for April immediately while she tried to shake off the worry that came from someone else possibly using her identity. Maybe it was just an oversight?

Nevertheless, April could hear the officer speaking into a device strapped to her shoulder. "One April Stephens arriving. I need a security check on an earlier female guest—"

Whatever else the guard said was lost to her ears as she stepped from the Land Rover and down onto the red carpet. There were no cameras here, but it was as lavish as any state receiving line. Liveried attendants greeted them warmly. A man took April's coat, a woman gave her a magnolia flower and explained to her how to find the ladies' lounge, the swag room and the bar. Instead of following any of those directions, however, she rejoined Weston, who'd been given a small card with an itinerary for the evening.

He pocketed it and led her out of the wide foyer toward a sprawling front room with couches, a fireplace and a bar tucked in the front corner. She guessed there were about thirty people milling around while the catering staff passed through with trays of hors d'oeuvres.

"There's a swag room?" April whispered, even though they weren't close enough to anyone to be overheard.

She checked her hair in a hallway mirror, but her gaze was more drawn to the man beside her. Dressed for a black-tie event, he bore little resemblance to the surly rancher who'd once told her he'd have her escorted off the property if she kept asking questions. And he didn't even look like the mountaineering rescuer who'd spent the night with her on Trapper Peak. Tonight, in his black silk bow tie and sleekly cut jacket, Weston looked every inch the mogul. He could blend seamlessly into the world beyond the double doors because he was one of them, a man born to wealth and privilege, even if he'd worked hard to give back in his life. She was starting to think maybe she could blend in too.

He moved closer to her to reply, and her focus hitched on the image of the two of them together in the mirror. "We invited most of the guests here tonight to get them excited about the guest ranch amenities. The more they invest their time and energy in environmental projects, the more we want to support them. Their influencer status can propel our efforts forward faster than any ad placement."

The reminder of the ranch's high profile—and their reliance on a positive public image to grow their good works—forced her to think about how a connection to a hoarder might hurt that. Her mother's rampant consumerism felt like the antithesis of what a sustainable environment like this was all about. Even if April fit into his world, the last thing she wanted to do was hurt him.

"So you woo them with swag?" she teased, if only to redirect her unhappy thoughts.

Someone turned the music up inside the great room. The song had a retro vibe, but the singer was someone modern. Two women perched near each other on the edge of a coffee table jumped up and started grooving, champagne glasses in hand.

"Absolutely we do." His hand slid to the center of her back, a warm weight that both comforted her and tantalized her. "Are you ready to go in?"

She'd been stalling, perhaps. Licking her lips, she was about to say yes when she remembered one more thing.

"I haven't seen my new friend here yet." She leaned toward the great room doors, peering into the farthest corner of the space where it melded into an informal dining area and a kitchen. "We met at a fitting—"

A commotion erupted near the front door as a social media star with her own makeup brand stepped into the foyer with an entourage of at least fifteen that multiplied before their eyes. Even the other celebrities—the pop singer, the soap opera star, a duo from an international boy band—all had their phones out to record the woman's arrival.

April sidled closer to Weston, gripping his arm as more guests came from the great room to see what was going on in the foyer. The woman—Chiara Campagna—was accepting a magnolia flower from the greeter while a hubbub ensued all around her.

Weston slid his arm fully around her waist, keeping her near him. A strikingly tall man in a tuxedo appeared on April's other side, his burly shoulders brushing her as he leaned in to say something quietly to Weston.

"This is more than we planned for, mate. We need more security." The man spoke in an accent that might be Australian. He smiled down at April as he eased back an inch. "I'm Gage, by the way."

"April Stephens," she replied. "And thank you for inviting me. Your home is beautiful."

"Thank you." He gave her a rueful look. "I know this isn't everyone's idea of a party, though, love. Come back in the summer when we can kick our shoes off, barbecue some ribs and throw horseshoes by the pool. That's more my speed."

Gage's dark eyes returned to the crowded foyer, a furrow of worry etched in his forehead. He had thick brown hair and the physique of a professional wrestler. Hints of intricate tattoos emerged from one sleeve when he moved.

He wasn't what she'd imagined when she'd envisioned Weston's private school friends, which said something about her preconceived notions. She ducked out of the way of one of the catering wait-staff taking video of Chiara Campagna while the star took a selfie with the two members of the boy band. Her bodyguards were never far from her.

Leaning forward to speak to Gage, Weston said, "I need all the help I can get convincing April to spend more time here."

Flattered, April wondered if he was serious about that. He hadn't said anything about wanting to continue a relationship after she left. It seemed impossible, and yet…a tiny hope sparked inside her even though she'd told herself she would not allow that to happen tonight.

Gage nodded, his dark eyes still monitoring the front door as if he was worried about a security threat. "Definitely spend a while with us when there's not so much hype." He snapped his fingers suddenly, turning toward April again. "April. You're the financial forensics investigator. How's your case going?"

All the hopeful feelings she'd been having fell away as she remembered the news she hadn't shared with Weston yet. It had been a topic she'd hoped to avoid awhile longer, but that didn't mean she'd lie about it.

"It's closed," she told him, feeling Weston tense beside her, his fingers clenching slightly against the fabric of her dress. "I've tracked enough of Alonzo's earnings to satisfy my client, so I'm officially finished with my work at Mesa Falls." She turned to meet Weston's gaze, knowing that what she had to say would mean more to him. To them. Taking a deep breath, she took ownership of her decision, reminding herself that he'd only intended for this to be short term too. "I'll be flying back to Denver tomorrow."

Thirteen

Still reeling from April's revelation that her flight was already booked and that she had no intention of spending another moment beyond tonight with him, Weston grappled for a response. Especially here, in the foyer now jammed with excited guests.

If it hadn't come up now, when had she planned on telling him? On her way out the door? Or worse yet, not at all?

He ducked his head and whispered for her ears alone, "We need to talk. Privately."

He thought she nodded, because he felt her silky hair bob against his jaw. But as he turned her away from the throng of partygoers, he came face-to-face with the tabloid reporter dressed in strapless crimson silk and velvet, her dark hair half pinned up and half trailing down her back.

Gage's ex.

Weston couldn't imagine how she'd slipped past security. Until she opened her arms wide.

"April!" Elena Rollins folded his date into her embrace like they were old friends.

Gage shot him a furious glance over their heads. Weston wondered if April even knew that Elena held a phone in one hand, recording everything. And a throng of people stood in his way, preventing him from hustling April out the door.

"Smile for my followers," Elena instructed her as they eased apart, lifting her camera high overhead to get both of them in the shot.

April politely complied, but he could see the uneasiness in her expression. The moment of confusion.

"Were you unaware of Elena's day job?" Gage asked as he plucked the cell from the reporter's fingers, dropping it in the pocket of his jacket. "She's now a professional menace."

The shock on April's face might have made Weston feel sympathetic if he hadn't just been dealt a far worse blow himself.

"I'm so sorry," she said, blue eyes darting back and forth between Gage and Elena, who were now in a searing standoff.

"They don't even hear you," Weston told her, drawing her away from the dinner-party drama and toward a room in the back. "Unless, of course, you intended that apology for me." He picked up speed as they passed the library and Gage's office, seeking the small den toward the back of the house. April's heels tapped loudly on the hardwood-look tile as she kept up beside him. "In which case I don't accept it."

"Should you…help? Out there?" April glanced over her shoulder toward the party, but Weston closed the door to the den.

It was the smallest room in the overblown mansion, and Weston appreciated the coziness of the whitewashed log walls, reminding him no one was going to come out of the woodwork and surprise him—not paparazzi or other guests. It was just April and him. Photos from Gage's childhood were interspersed with histories and biographies on bookshelves that flanked a window overlooking the backyard.

"No. I've been running interference for them for weeks." Weston's head throbbed as he walked past the gray tweed sofa toward the window, but he was grateful for the pain since it helped him keep his mind off the ache in his chest. An ache that had started when April announced she was done in Montana. He knew that meant she was done with him, a rejection that hurt so much more than he would have expected. "I told them I needed help managing the fallout from the Tabitha Barnes announcement. Let them figure it out for a change."

"I had no idea Elena was the tabloid reporter." April fidgeted with one of the chiffon flowers on her dress, not moving any closer to him. She remained by an antique wingback near a grandfather clock. "It never occurred to me. She seemed so nice."

"I'm sure she is." Weston suspected she must have been very special to Gage at one time for the almighty Striker patriarch to see her as a threat to the family's image. "She just happens to have a job that can ruin us, and she's also got an ax to grind with Gage."

"She's so lovely, I just assumed she was one of the celebrity guests when she said she was attending the party tonight." Relinquishing the fabric bloom, she met his gaze, and he saw regret shimmering in her clear blue eyes. "We shared a dress fitting this afternoon and started talking. I'd never met her before today."

"It doesn't matter." Weston knew better than to concern himself with the drama Elena would stir. Gage would take over on that front. "What I care about is why you didn't tell me your case was closed. Why would you make plans to leave Mesa Falls without telling me?"

He turned to study her, already feeling the weight of her departure strangling all the plans he'd had for tonight.

She crossed her arms over her chest, her whole posture radiating a closed-off vibe. "I wanted to just enjoy what time we had."

"Enjoy it? You looked forward to counting down the minutes until you left." He was rattled and off his game from how fast the playing field was shifting under his feet. But it felt like she was purposely shredding all his hopes for creating something more. "No wonder you didn't take me up on an offer of climbing a foreign mountain range in time to see the sunrise. You knew you wouldn't be here."

"I should have told you sooner," she admitted, accepting the blame and meeting his eyes. "I'm sorry, Weston. But I've found it difficult to trust what I'm feeling when this is all happening so fast."

Damn right it was happening fast. He remained rooted to the spot, one shoulder against the window frame, even thought he'd rather be holding her.

"You're the one rushing to leave," he pointed out. "If you stayed, we could take our time. Explore what's happening—"

"I can't do that." She spread her hands wide in a gesture of hopelessness, her pink fingernails making him wish she had her hands on him. Touching him. "I have a life in Denver. I've never been away from home as long as I have for this case, and my mother's anxiety gets worse when I'm not around."

"So leave and come back." It seemed easy enough from where he was standing. Or at least it was if April really cared about him. If she was truly as moved as he was by their explosive connection. "I get being committed to family, April, but that doesn't help me understand why you won't consider continuing our relationship. It doesn't have to end just because you're leaving Mesa Falls."

He studied her expression, trying to understand her. But when she bit her lip, her gaze shifting, he had a flash of insight.

"Unless that's what you've been banking on all along," he continued, as he connected the dots. "Is the end of your work just an excuse to end things?"

Bitterness crept into his words. He heard it, and he guessed she did too.

"I can't afford to dig myself in any deeper." She moved closer to him, resting a tentative hand on his arm.

He noticed she didn't deny it. The sense of betrayal stung. "How long have you known you had no intention of seeing me once your investigation was finished?"

"I didn't think about it in those terms," she insisted. "I just knew if we spent any more time together this week…" She swallowed hard and looked away before meeting his gaze again, tears hovering on the edges of her eyelids. "I knew it would only make leaving more impossible than it already is."

"So don't do it." Frustration simmered as the touch of her hand stirred him, tempted him, reminded him of all he would lose when she left. It was a feeling more intense than he'd felt for any other woman. "When was the last time you took a risk, April?"

Snatching her hand back, her lips went tight. He recognized that flicker of pain in her pretty blue eyes. He remembered the pain she'd described when she'd done something she'd regretted as a teen.

"As an adult," he clarified. The last thing he wanted was to hurt her. "I know figuring things out with me might seem messy and complicated, but that doesn't mean it wouldn't be worth it."

"I don't understand." She shook her head, pacing away from him, her dress swishing against her calves. "What are you suggesting?"

He hesitated, her question catching him off guard.

"I'm not sure," he told her carefully, weighing his words, wanting to be truthful, which was tough to do when his gut was roiling with emotion. "Because I haven't had time to work that out. But I know there's something between us that deserves more time—"

She cut him off. "I can't pin my hopes on fragile possibilities that will only break my heart, Weston." Her chin trembled for a moment before she continued. "I've avoided falling for you because I know how painful it would be to lose something special like that."

"So you don't even try?" He couldn't believe his ears. Straightening from the window, he followed her to where she stood by the grandfather clock.

The damned ticking reminded him of everything that wasn't working between them, and that he was just counting down the seconds until he lost her.

"I'm not like you, Weston." She held herself very straight, as if touching him again might shatter her. "I've never been the one who jumped in with both feet. I need to weigh my decisions. To think through the outcomes—"

"All of which requires time. And you've already said you won't give that to me."

He knew then that he was fighting a losing battle. Tilting at windmills. That she didn't see him the way he saw her. And she'd been plotting her exit strategy all week long.

The grandfather clock chimed the half hour, startling her when she'd been standing so close. It didn't surprise him, though. He'd known this was coming from the moment they'd walked into the room. Dragging in a long breath, he said, "Clearly nothing I have to say is going to change your mind."

How had he tangled himself up with a woman who would never take a chance? He'd spent too long being the wildcard in his family to enter into a relationship with a woman who viewed him that way too.

Not that she was giving him a chance.

"You'll be happier without me in the long run." She held her magnolia flower in a death grip, one of the petals floating to the floor.

"Do me a favor, and don't pretend to know what's best for me." He didn't bother to hide the resentment in his voice, the thought of walking away from her stirring an ache unlike anything he'd ever felt before.

April's blue gaze remained steady. "Goodbye, Weston."

Bitterness and betrayal warred inside him.

When she slipped out the door, he knew his life wasn't ever going to be the same again without her.

* * *

Weston had no idea what time it was when the door to the den opened again. At first, he pried his eyes open, disoriented as he realized he must have fallen asleep since he hadn't wanted to rejoin the party.

When the door slammed hard enough to rattle the windows, he bolted straight up from his spot on the sofa.

His brother stopped in the middle of the room.

"Wes?" Miles flicked on a reading lamp near the wingback. "What the hell are you doing in here?"

Blinking from the sudden brightness, Weston scraped a hand through his hair, his eyes gritty, his insides still raw from April's rejection.

"Sulking." He'd laid his tux jacket over the arm of the sofa and had been using it for a pillow. A half-empty glass of scotch sat on the cocktail table nearby.

He hadn't felt like drinking after April left, but he didn't know what else to do. Half a glass had been enough to help him sleep for a few minutes. Or maybe it had been a few hours. He didn't know.

Miles reached for the glass and sniffed it. "This any good?"

"Judge for yourself," he muttered.

"Does the sulking have anything to do with the pretty blonde you came with?" He downed the drink in one gulp, then dropped onto the opposite end of the sofa and put his feet on the cocktail table. "I saw her leave alone a couple of hours ago."

Damn it. He'd slept longer than he thought, and he still didn't have any answers for what to say to April to smooth things over. Having Miles here made him remember how much he missed having friends— bonds that went beyond keeping secrets. He and Miles had had that, once.

So he found himself confiding.

"I messed things up, and I don't even know how." He regretted that he hadn't measured his words more carefully, but he didn't think that would have made the end result any different.

"Want me to help you figure it out?" Miles offered, loosening his tie and then pitching it on the floor.

Something was definitely wrong with his brother if he of all people was offering relationship advice. They'd always been so different. Miles had never understood Weston's restlessness, his need to do more than just work a ranch. Their paths had made them both successful, just in very different ways.

"What gives?" Weston narrowed his gaze, trying to see what he'd missed. "Since when do you do the hard work for me? Haven't you always been the one pushing for me to buckle down and focus, to figure it out for myself?"

"According to you, I'm the model son, right? I can do no wrong. Maybe I just need five minutes of feeling like I have all the answers you think I do." The dark scowl on Miles's brow was familiar enough from Weston's own glimpses in the mirror, but he couldn't recall ever seeing the expression on his older sibling's face.

He had zero experience helping his brother, but he had to at least offer. To try.

"Miles—"

"Give me this, okay?" he asked more quietly. Less aggressively. "Being with all the guys again…it's like I hear Zach in my ear. I need to do something else, okay? So tell me, why did she leave you?"

Weston understood all too well. He spilled out the story about April as well as he could, understanding now why she hadn't given him any time or preparation, that she'd kept him in the dark about her departure right up until tonight. She'd never had any intention of giving them a fighting chance to work things out between them. She'd always planned on using her work as an excuse to shut things down.

"Do you love her?" Miles asked when Weston was finished, picking at the button cover on his shirt.

"Love?" The word stopped him short. Weston hadn't thought in those terms. "I haven't known her that long."

"Bullshit." Miles never even looked up from flicking the button cover. "You know you love April, or at the very least are well on your way to falling for her. I can hear it in your voice when you talk about her."

He loved April? The feeling flooded him. Filled him. Hell yes, he loved her. He'd never thought about any woman day and night before, never spent days figuring out how to woo someone. He'd had a plane on standby tonight just in case she took him up on that offer to go to Paris or anywhere else she chose. More than anything, he wanted her to be happy. And if that wasn't love, he didn't know the first thing about it.

Then he remembered she was leaving. And all of this might be a moot point. His chest got tight again.

"But if I tell her that—"

Miles sat up and focused his gaze on him for the first time since he'd entered the room. "With all due respect, I'm going to go out on a limb and say that April sounds like she has more in common with someone like me. Sounds like she has the kind of character you think I have—logical, cautious, thoughtful."

"I'd hardly compare her to you," he said drily, thinking of her soft hair. Her scent. Curves he wanted to touch all the time. But it was true that April had a more reserved nature than Weston did.

They balanced each other.

"Okay. But she's not like you. You save people. You take chances. And everyone loves you for that." There was a wealth of bitterness in those words. "People like you can fall in love fast, and that's fine. But someone like April might not feel as…free…to do the same. Maybe she has too much responsibility weighing her down to do something so…romantic." He spat out the word with particular distaste. "My guess is she needs you to take the leap. To do what you do best."

Weston felt like a hole had opened up under his feet. He'd fallen into an upside-down world where Miles made sense and understood him. Where Miles seemed to almost envy him.

On the one hand, he wanted to figure out what was going on with his brother, because even someone as illogical as Weston apparently was wise to the fact that Miles was hurting like hell. But on the other hand, he also knew that you didn't poke a hurt animal with a stick, so he'd have to figure out an approach another time.

Besides, the need to talk to April, to possibly stop her before she caught her flight back home, was propelling him to his feet even now. He didn't know if he could persuade her, but he had to try or he would regret it for the rest of his life. And he knew firsthand from losing his best friend how deeply regrets could cripple a person.

"I don't know how you knew that. Any of that," he confessed as he punched his arms through the sleeves of his tux jacket. "But you're right. I do love her."

A wry smile curved his brother's lips. "Go get her, Wes."

Weston hesitated by the door. "You need anything?"

The grandfather clock said it was 2:00 a.m. How the hell had he fallen asleep for that long?

"Nah," he said quietly, falling back on the sofa as if he was going to take over the spot to sleep. "Thanks for letting me do one good thing today."

"Thank you, brother. I owe you." Switching off the lamp, Weston closed the door behind him. Now he needed to find April. And pray like hell that Miles was, indeed, as smart as Weston thought he was. Because if he could fix this, Weston owed him everything.

The only good news in the last twenty-four hours was that her bag was still packed with her climbing gear.

April had checked and double-checked the weather report for Trapper Peak before starting her predawn trek, confident that this time no storms were blowing in. Conditions were good on the mountain, even for someone without much winter climbing experience. She wasn't going to summit. She was just headed for Gem Lake, the same place she'd hiked the first time she'd come to Montana before Christmas.

The destination wouldn't have as many memories for her as the other path—the one that had led her to spend that first night in Weston's arms. The thought of that night—and the devastating ending to her time with him at the party the evening before—threatened to bring her to her knees. The hurt was an actual physical pain in her body that made it harder, slower to climb. She'd been the one who'd set the terms. The one to insist their time together had a limit. So why did it hurt so much now?

She kept climbing despite the hurt in her chest, not knowing any other way to pass the rest of the hours in Montana before her afternoon flight. She *needed* to do something or she would go crazy from the hurt and loss that had come with all of her poor choices. She couldn't believe she'd never feel Weston's arms around her again.

Or sleep in his bed.

Now, as the first hint of sunrise stole over the mountain, she paused to savor the pink tinge to the snow. She curled her toes inside her boots and breathed in the mountain air, wishing it could heal the hurt inside her, that it would clear her mind as it had in the past. But even with the delicate dance of pink light turning to tangerine, the surprise spotting of a rabbit hopping just off her path, she couldn't ease the ache inside her.

Was she wrong to close her heart to hope?

The bird wheeling over her head right now, calling and cawing, seemed to think so. With all of the mountainside waking up now, it felt like a crime against nature to not celebrate the start to a new day. A new start. A tender beginning.

When had she become so cowardly?

She set her backpack down on the ground, unzipping it to find a water bottle and take a drink. She needed to fuel up and replenish, to go back down the mountain and tell Weston she'd made a mistake.

Drinking so fast that some sloshed on her cheek, April righted the water bottle and blinked at what she saw in her peripheral vision.

A broad-shouldered hiker trekking up the mountain right toward her.

Squinting into the orangey-yellow glow behind the figure, she felt her heart swell with happiness as she recognized the figure.

Weston. He'd come after her. Come for her. Even after she'd pushed him away, he hadn't given up on her. And that spoke volumes.

Shoving her water bottle back in her bag, she charged toward him.

"Weston?" she called to him even though she knew him almost right away.

She recognized his dark winter parka. His climbing gear. His long hair curling up under the sides of his cap.

He lifted his snow goggles to stare up at her with his hazel eyes.

She shuffled to a stop, her heart overcome with emotions she didn't know how to put into words. For all that she wanted to tell him she was sorry, that she'd made a mistake, she was still feeling overwhelmed that he had found her at dawn in the most unlikely of places.

"How did you know I was here?" she asked when he slowed to a stop a foot in front of her. Close enough to touch, their cloudy breaths mingling in the space between them.

She tried to read his expression, hoping that he would give her a chance to explain the things she'd been too tongue-tied and uncertain about the night before. She'd missed him so much this week. Not just last night, but every night before that when she'd tried to put up walls between them. To keep herself from falling for him. Which was so foolish of her, when she already had.

"You left word with the ranch manager and the front desk, like a good climber should," he explained, peeling off his gloves and shoving them in the pocket of his jacket.

The weather was still cold, but the climb could warm a body up.

"You went to the lodge?"

He must have gone there long before dawn for him to be here now. She studied him closer in the morning sunlight, noticing the shadowed bristle along his jaw. She wanted to tuck herself into the hard planes of his body and stay there.

"I went looking for you a little after two o'clock once I figured out that I love you." He clasped her arms in a tender grip, his gaze steady on hers. "I needed you to know that before you left. For whatever it's worth."

Her brain turned all of his words after "I love you" to static. She couldn't hear anything else.

"You love me?" She wanted to tell him so many things. How she was on her way down the mountain to tell him she was wrong. That she wanted another chance.

But her heart beat so loudly it filled her ears and

made her legs weak. Tears stung her eyes, but they were the good kind.

"I love you, April," he repeated slowly, stepping closer to her so he could slide his hand around the back of her neck, stroking her there lightly with his thumb. "I appreciate that you might think it's too soon to feel that way. But I know it's true, and I need you to know that you mean everything to me. I realize you will need time. Just please don't give up on us. Give me the opportunity to show you how good we can be together. Forever."

"Oh. Weston." She tipped her head against his, breathing in his presence, his love, his certainty. She envied him his ability to be so at peace with feelings that had terrified her when she'd feared they wouldn't be returned. "I'm so sorry I didn't give us a chance last night. I've been holding all my own feelings at bay this week, scared they'd level me faster than any avalanche if I acknowledged them. But it was so foolish of me when the feelings were there anyway, silently killing me from the inside out."

"You're so much tougher than you know." He kissed her face, and it was even more beautiful than sunrise on a mountain, the best sort of fresh start that she could imagine.

"I think I got tangled up by needing all the answers before I could allow myself to feel like this was real." She tucked her head into his chest for a long moment, feeling his heartbeat there, steadying her. Grounding her.

"You deserve to have answers. And I can't wait to figure them out with you so they all add up."

She glanced up to find him smiling down at her. Teasing her gently.

"I wasn't always this way, so afraid," she whispered against his jaw, kissing him there.

"You're strong and brave. Just cautious. And that's okay. I love you just the way you are." He cupped her chin in one hand, a breeze stirring the snow around them like a snow globe, the sun glittering on the icy bits. "And it just so happens I brought the key to a cabin the ranch owns near Gem Lake." He produced a key card from his jacket pocket and held it up for her to see. "What do you say we head over there and work on our plans for the next few weeks?"

She was so tempted. More than anything, she wanted to retreat to a cabin on the mountainside with him. Preferably for days. "My mother expects me home tonight. I feel like I should check in."

"Of course you should," he agreed, brushing a touch along her cheek and then following it with a kiss. "But I didn't have the chance to tell you that the ranch has a private airstrip that makes flights really simple. And fast. We can still go to the cabin and spend the day there. After dinner, I'll make sure you get to Denver for however long you need to be there."

April's heart turned over for this man, touched that he accepted how much she still wanted to be there for her mother, to help her on her journey to recover one day. "Thank you for understanding. And yes, I'd love to visit this cabin with you."

For days, she'd craved his touch and denied herself the pleasure, fearing that she'd fall hopelessly in love with him. Now, she could fall as far, as deeply, as she wanted.

She couldn't wait.

"You're going to love the view," he promised her, tucking her under one arm.

"That's not all I'm going to love." Stopping, she arched up on her toes to kiss his lips.

A long, lingering kiss that tasted like forever.

* * * * *

*Will Elena take her revenge on Gage
with a hit piece about Mesa Falls?*

Find out in
Heartbreaker,
coming in March 2020!

*Dynasties: Mesa Falls
Don't miss a single installment!*

The Rebel
The Rival
Rule Breaker
Heartbreaker
The Rancher
The Heir

by USA TODAY *bestselling author
Joanne Rock*

*Available exclusively
from Harlequin Desire.*

*Gage Striker vows to protect Mesa Falls Ranch from
prying paparazzi at any cost—even when the press includes
his former lover, Elena Rollins. Past misunderstandings
fuel current tempers, but will this fire between them
reignite their attraction?*

Read on for a sneak peek of
Heartbreaker
by USA TODAY bestselling author Joanne Rock

Elena Rollins stepped toward him, swathed in strapless crimson silk and velvet. Her dark hair was half pinned up and half trailing down her back, a few glossy curls spilling over one bare shoulder. Even now, six years later, she took his breath away as fast as a punch to his chest. For a single devastating instant, he thought the smile curving her red lips was for him.

Then she opened her arms wide.

"April!" Elena greeted Weston Rivera's date warmly, wrapping her in a one-armed embrace like they were old friends.

Only then did Gage notice how Elena gripped her phone in her other hand, holding it out at arm's length to record everything. Was it a live video? Anger surged through him at the same time he wondered how in the hell she knew April Stephens.

"Were you unaware of Elena's day job?" Gage asked April as he plucked the device from Elena's red talons and dropped it in the pocket of his tuxedo jacket. "She's now a professional menace."

Elena rounded on him, pinning him with her dark eyes. They stood deadlocked in fuming silence. "That belongs to me," Elena sniped, tipping her chin at him. "You have no right to take it."

"You have no right to be here, but I see you didn't let that stop you from finagling your way onto the property."

She glared at him, dark eyes narrowing. "My video is probably still recording. Maybe you should return my phone before you cause a scene that will bring you bad press."

Extending a palm, she waited for him to hand it over.

"If you have a problem with me, why don't you tell it to the security team you tricked into admitting you tonight?" He pointed toward the door, where two bodyguards in gray suits were stationed on either side of the entrance. "You're trespassing."

"Is that a dare, Gage?" Her voice hit a husky note, no doubt carefully calibrated to distract a man.

It damn well wasn't going to work on him.

"I'm giving you a choice," he clarified, unwilling to give her the public showdown she so clearly wanted to record and share with her followers. "You can speak with me privately about whatever it is you're doing in my house, or you can let my team escort you off the premises right now. Either way, I can promise you there won't be any cameras involved."

"How positively boring." She gave him a tight smile and a theatrical sigh before folding her arms across her chest. "Maybe using cameras could spice things up a bit."

She gave him a once-over with her dark gaze.

He reminded himself that if she got under his skin, she won. But he couldn't deny a momentary impulse to kiss her senseless for trying to play him.

"What will it be, Elena?" he pressed, keeping his voice even. "Talk or walk?"

"Very well." She gestured with her hands, holding them up in a sign of surrender. "Spirit me away to your lair, Gage, and do with me what you will." She tipped her head to one side, a thoughtful expression stealing across her face. "Oh, wait a minute." She bit her lip and shook her head. "You don't indulge your bad-boy side anymore, do you? Your father saw to that a long time ago, paying off all the questionable influences to leave his precious heir alone."

The seductive, playful note in her voice was gone, a cold chill stealing into her gaze.

He'd known she had an ax to grind with him after the way his father had bribed her to get out of his life.

He hadn't realized how hard she'd come out swinging.

Don't miss what happens next in
Heartbreaker
by Joanne Rock, part of her Dynasties: Mesa Falls series!

Available March 2020 wherever
Harlequin Desire books and ebooks are sold.

Harlequin.com

Love Harlequin romance?

DISCOVER.

Be the first to find out about promotions,
news and exclusive content!

 Facebook.com/HarlequinBooks

 Twitter.com/HarlequinBooks

 Instagram.com/HarlequinBooks

 Pinterest.com/HarlequinBooks

ReaderService.com

EXPLORE.

Sign up for the Harlequin e-newsletter and
download a free book from any series at
TryHarlequin.com

CONNECT.

Join our Harlequin community to
share your thoughts and connect
with other romance readers!
Facebook.com/groups/HarlequinConnection